FRANZ WERFEL

Pale Blue Ink
in a Lady's Hand

A NOVELLA

Translated from the German
by James Reidel

A Verba Mundi Book

David R. Godine · Publisher · Boston

This is a *Verba Mundi* Book
published in 2012 by
DAVID R. GODINE · *Publisher*
Post Office Box 450
Jaffrey, New Hampshire 03452
www.godine.com

Original title: *Eine blaßblaue Frauenschrift*
Copyright © 1955 by Alma Mahler-Werfel.
All rights reserved by S. Fischer Verlag GmbH, Frankfurt am Main.
English translation copyright © 2011 by James Reidel
The translator wishes to thank the National Endowment for the Arts
for making this translation possible.

LIBRARY OF CONGRESS CATALOGING-IN-PUBLICATION DATA

Werfel, Franz, 1890–1945.
[Blassblaue frauenschrift. English]
Pale blue ink in a lady's hand : a novel / by Franz Werfel ; translated
from the German by James Reidel.
p. cm.
"Originally published as Eine blaßblaue Frauenschrift."
ISBN 978-1-56792-408-4 (pbk.)
1. Married men—Fiction. 2. Jewish women—Fiction. 3. Triangles
(Interpersonal relations)—Fiction. I. Reidel, James. II. Title.
PT2647.E77B513 2012
833'.912—dc22
2010033435

FIRST PRINTING
Printed in the United States of America

PALE BLUE INK IN A LADY'S HAND

Also by Franz Werfel from David R. Godine

THE FORTY DAYS OF MUSA DAGH
Translated by Geoffrey Dunlop
and James Reidel

Franz Werfel's *Pale Blue Ink in a Lady's Hand* is a tale of interwar Austria and "unbreathable air," pointing to the gas and the ovens to come. It has that prescience of the Holocaust that Werfel saw in the Armenian Genocide and wrote about in his longest novel, *The Forty Days of Musa Dagh.* Werfel is still well known for that book about the resistance to the Turkish deportations and massacres during the First World War, which he intended as a premonition, a warning to German readers in 1933 of what their people could inflict on another. He is remembered too for *The Song of Bernadette* (1942), his novelization of Bernadette Soubirous's visions of the Blessed Virgin Mary in a grotto near the French town of Lourdes in 1858 and the Oscar-winning film that came of it. And he will be remembered for this novel as well, published here as a book and in a complete English translation for the first time.

A century has passed since Franz Werfel (1890–1945) published his first poems in the feuilletons of Viennese newspapers and his first book of Expressionist verse, *Der Weltfreund* in 1911. The title means the "world friend," "friend of the world," even "philanthropist" – a noble and self-consciously impossible task for the Prague-born Jew who felt comfortably assimilated and estranged in the same person.

The book enjoyed much acclaim, and Werfel went on to publish more poems, plays, novels, and essays. By the mid-1930s, when *Pale Blue Ink in a Lady's Hand* takes place, Werfel had a biographer, was rumored to be in consideration for the Nobel Prize, and seemed destined to rank with Dostoevsky and Tolstoy. His success, especially given his incredible royalties and fees during the Depression years and his seeming betrayal of modernism, earned him many young detractors, such as Elias Canetti, whose Vienna memoirs reveal Werfel at his height and the opprobrium that would be shoveled on him after his death.

The Armenian Christians and Roman Catholics still revere *their* novels and admire how a Jewish-Austrian writer had given voice to a national tragedy and rendered such a loving portrait of simple piety. Jews, however, lacked such a book; and given their portrayals in the rest of his opus, it reinforced the view that Werfel was not just assimilated. He was to many a Jew in name only and represented others like him, indeed, a small but influential percentage of his readership. But he differed from them in becoming the "leading literary *homo religiosus* of his age" – a living experiment in comparative religion that began when his Czech Catholic nurse took him to mass. It continued with his education at a Piarist Fathers school, where a visiting rabbi came for his bar mitzvah studies. As a young poet, Werfel dabbled in theosophy and the occult, attending Max Brod's Prague séances, which sometimes included their friend, Franz Kafka. Some of these contemporaries saw Werfel increasingly as a *crypto-Catholic* rather than a fellow Jew, or a fusion of the two faiths. Trumping these, however, woven into his fiction, poems, and plays, was matriarchy, the mother goddess, the priestess, concepts reinforced by his café society mentor, the renegade psychoanalyst-addict Otto Gross. In 1917 Werfel found a pagan savior in Alma Mahler, his "Midday Goddess" (and her daughters' "*Tigermami*"), the widow of the composer Gustav Mahler, the lover of Oskar Kokoschka (who painted her as the *Bride of the Wind*), and still the wife of the Bauhaus founder Walter Gropius. Werfel became the next genius she would cultivate, and her third husband.

In February 1940, Werfel started drafting what he called an "intricate little tale of a marriage." He now lived in exile in the south of France following Austria's incorporation into the Third Reich. He was in Capri when that happened. He had missed the *Putzkolonnen*, the brush brigades of Jews who had to wash off the patriotic Austrian slogans chalked on Vienna's sidewalks, missed seeing the formerly patriotic Austrians change into loyal Nazis, and missed being sent to Dachau himself. He had tried to write a *Zeitroman* about such experiences, which would be his first real contribution to exile literature. But he could not finish it – and a heart attack suffered in Paris had made it harder as he recovered, living and working in a medieval watchtower near the resort of Sanary-sur-Mer during that ominously temporary respite, the Phoney War of early 1940, when Hitler seemed to have been stopped by France's Maginot Line.

What Werfel had in mind would be set in the recent past, a past that seemed eons ago to him, that time of the Austro-Fascists and their so-called *Ständestaat*, the doomed corporate state modeled after Mussolini's Italy that lasted from 1934 to 1938. Yet Austria during this time was also a place of exile for Jews fleeing Nazi Germany following the Nuremberg

Laws, and it offered a brief window on what was to come. This in part was probably what he meant when he told his publisher, Gottfried Fischer, that the new book was something that he "had never tried before," something "tricky." After a working title of indecision on how and when to begin – *Entanglements of an October Day,... of an April Day* – Werfel settled on *Eine blaßblaue Frauenschrift*, literally "a pale-blue lady's handwriting."

The style itself was not untried. Werfel had written social commentaries in the *Jung-Wien* tradition, and his little tale parodied a day in the life of Section Chief Leonidas, an Austrian career civil servant and an emblem of the country he served. His Spartan hero's name is a play on that Catholic Austria's meme of being a stopgap against the vulgarians of the East, whether they be the Turks of old, the Russians, Prussians, Bolsheviks, and now, very tactfully, a former Austrian who now ran Germany from Berlin.

Because much of Werfel's worldview was shaped by the theater and opera – he sang a good party tenor for Alma's salon – he tended to cast the lead roles, cameos, and even supernumeraries of his novels with people he knew. Thus, for the character of Leonidas, Werfel hardly disguised the name of Leodegar Petrin, a real-life section chief at the Ministry for Culture and Education, who served the Austrian state during the 1920s and '30s. He was certainly known to Werfel, and they appear in a volume of photographs for the official attendees at a gala concert to celebrate the centenary of Beethoven's death in March 1927. For Leonidas's wife, Amelie, Werfel was more nuanced in her makeup, as he would be with the novel's other wronged woman, and this may have been the "tricky" issue he mentioned to his publisher. Amelie is surely informed by Petrin's younger first wife, Melitta, the daughter of Adolf Lichtenfeld, an authority on Franz Grillparzer – and by whatever lost and intimate story exists between her and Petrin's rise. The Amelie character, however, is a composite. Her being a wealthy Paradini, a name redolent of the suburban paradise she provides Leonidas (whose own surname is unnecessary to the story), and a society Olympian to the husband she has made a minor god, reveals how both the early and late Alma make up Amelie. Their names suggest the connection, and Alma was once an Austrian trophy wife and a beauty who considered herself "Aryan" (much to the dismay of her Jewish husbands, Mahler and Werfel). But where Alma was this comely fin-de-siècle muse with a complete set of Nietzsche, Amelie is updated. Her modern (and seeming) superficiality is what makes her the *über-*, the superwoman, never bearing children and pursuing a regimen of grapefruit diets, gymnastics, and grueling hair appointments under a nickel-plated hair-dryer that blows so hot with her desire to keep her age and husband in check that the resulting set of her hair could almost be the helmet of Athena or a valkyrie. She represents one state of woman for Werfel and for Leonidas.

The other state is represented in the woman Leonidas betrays, the "love of his life," Vera Wormser, whose name means truth. The two bouquets Leonidas attempts to give her in *Pale Blue Ink* are reprises, or, more to Werfel's point, an eternal recurrence of impotence, not the power Nietzsche meant. These bouquets date to the spring of 1905, when Werfel was a schoolboy infatuated with Marie Immisch, a celebrated actress in Prague's German-language theater. During the city's May Festival, she played the title role in Schiller's *Maria Stuart*. Werfel saw her from the cheap seats of the balcony and was imprinted for a lifetime:

"Her hair was black. Her eyes were blue. / She played girl, child, and lady / . . . She was my dear and holy faith, / The one who pierced the invulnerable me." "Six Septets to Honor the Spring of 1905" goes on to describe how the boy Werfel tried to present the *Salondame* with a bouquet of flowers, but, upon seeing her leave the theater with a wealthy lover, froze in his tracks and said nothing. Then he ran away into a nearby park and tossed his flowers into a pond. From that point on, he believed he had been presented with his life's path – to be a writer and worthy of such a woman – but with the realization that she would be unattainable – "That we only get what we never get." But the actress is just one in a series of unattainable women, including Mitzi Glaser, the Prague girl with the tennis racket in another poem, who took no notice of him.

Vera comes from these women and is another *Verkörperung der weiblichen Magie*, that is, the "personification of female magic" as Wolfgang Paulsen terms Werfel's obsession-method.* Max Brod described her as unique among Werfel's other Jewish characters, which are more often the "broken Jewish type." She is "aware of her dignity with a sound mind, all the while circumspect, subtle, tolerantly forgiving, and, above all, beautiful, bewitching." Vera, too, has a "noble bearing," that of "intellect as well as sensibility," and a single-mindedness that is also "selfless, immune to insult . . ." For Werfel, certainly, she is that and what is different about the book, at least in one sense, given his early hints to his publisher. And it was written before his legions of Christian readers got their grotto, saint, and virgin. This Jewish "grotto,"

---

* Wolfgang Paulsen, *Franz Werfel: Sein Weg in den Roman* [Franz Werfel: His Method in the Novel] (Tübingen: Francke, 1995).

is perfectly clear when Vera makes her brief appearance in a Viennese hotel lounge, a chthonic place like Lourdes, with a bad jazz band in the background.

There is another source for Vera, too: Werfel's step-daughter Manon Gropius, called "Mutzi," Alma's daughter with Gropius. Manon wanted to be an actress, and, as a very young child, was particularly fond of a scene from Werfel's play *Mirror Man*, in which she'd play both the father, asking, "Where's my child?" and the mother, answering: "You're standing at its grave!" In adolescence, Manon took on the appearance, too, of Werfel's Prague beauties, with long dark hair parted in the middle and hanging past her waist. She had blue-gray eyes, a pale complexion, a slim figure, and a darker voice and wit compared to other girls. When the great impresario Max Reinhardt saw her, he asked Werfel if he could cast her as the First Angel in the revival of Hugo von Hofmannsthal's *The Great Theater of the World* for the Salzburg Festival of 1934. Werfel angrily disallowed it because the role required an experienced actress.

Not long after Reinhardt's offer, during the Easter holiday of 1934, Manon contracted polio and was bedridden, lingering for a year until she died on Easter Monday 1935. Werfel promised himself he would not "lose" her or see her go to "waste," and began working her life and death into his fiction from that point on (which is to say she is not just the revenant in Alban Berg's *Violin Concerto* dedicated to the "memory of an angel.")

One other ghost haunts *Pale Blue Ink in a Lady's Hand*. The boy described in Vera's letter and final speech is Werfel's reimagined infant son, Martin Johannes, the lovechild Alma bore in 1918. The child's early death haunts Werfel's writing work as intensely as the death of Manon.

Werfel finished the novel in April 1940, and in May Hitler invaded France through Belgium. An American agent for the European Rescue Committee, Varian Fry, facilitated the Werfels' escape from France. During this adventure, Werfel stayed in the shrine city of Lourdes and saw it as a factor in the miracle of his survival from the Nazis. Feeling indebted, but really taking up a theme in the first novel he tried to write about Manon, Werfel promised to write the story of St. Bernadette. This novel took precedence when he and Alma settled in southern California, where many creative German-speaking émigrés had gone, attracted by the chance to work in Hollywood and rebuild some approximation of the lives and careers they had in Europe.

Nevertheless, the manuscript of *Pale Blue Ink in a Lady's Hand* had found its way to the Jewish exile press, Editorial Estrellas, the publishing house of the *Jüdische Wochenschau* (The Jewish Weekly) in Buenos Aires. Werfel had had contacts in Argentina, fellow Jews going into exile, even Austro-Fascist bureaucrats deemed unacceptable by the Nazis and facing arrest themselves. Among them were the very models for those younger bureaucrats in the novella who annoy Leonidas, including Manon's alleged "fiancé" during her illness who asked Werfel and Alma if they could intercede on his behalf and find editorial work or a newspaper job for him in the exile press. Werfel's motivations for this venue are unknown, but it would seem that this book, which dealt directly with the victims of fascism, anti-Semitism, exile, even assimilation, would confuse an American audience accustomed to his spirituality, his semblance of Christian faith.

Title page from the first edition, published in Buenos Aires, 1941

The first edition of *Pale Blue Ink in a Lady's Hand* was published in German in early 1941. The reception among a largely Jewish readership must have heartened Werfel. Since the Book-of-the-Month Club, long a reliable source of income, had yet to buy *The Song of Bernadette*, he allowed Friedrich Torberg, a fellow exile more familiar with Hollywood, to adapt the novella for the screen in the fall of 1941. *Casablanca* was in production, and storylines about the fall of France had a market – why not one about Austria's fall? But Torberg knew better and the screenplay had nothing to do with that strange land. Leonidas was renamed Chester, a State Department diplomat. Amelie became the daughter of an isolationist senator. And the vaguely lesbian Vera in *Pale Blue* had been completely reworked into Helen, a scheming, emotional Frenchwoman. Walter Pidgeon, Mary Astor, and

Ida Lupino were under consideration for the starring roles, and the troubling theme of anti-Semitism evaporated into a light comedy about the wiles of getting an American visa. The director Robert Siodmak showed some interest in the treatment titled *April in October*, but passed on it, as did others.

With Pearl Harbor, war stories that lacked a real relevance to the war and patriotism had little chance of being produced as films or even books. The notable exception was *The Song of Bernadette* (1942), Werfel's Catholic novel – or "fairytale" as envious, fellow exiles called it. Werfel and his agent expected their new bestseller to have coattails when *The Song of Bernadette* came out as a film in 1943 and was nominated for numerous Oscars in 1944. But there were no coattails for *April in October* either as a book or film. At last an abridged translation, more like a long sentimental short story, ran in the February 1944 issue of *American Magazine*, a forgotten competitor of the *New Yorker*. Much had been cut and scrubbed clean, especially the *Lolita*-like fascination that Leonidas has for his nymphette, the traveling seduction, and the imaginary trial. The themes of anti-Semitism had also been softened and self-censored.

A year after this first English abridgement came and went, Werfel died, and his work fell precipitously out of fashion following the war. Thus, it would take decades before it was rediscovered in the 1970s, when Werfel's bones were reburied in Vienna and he enjoyed a rediscovery. One book that contributed to his renaissance among German and Austrian readers was *Pale Blue Ink in a Lady's Hand*. In addition to standing out from the rest of Werfel's œuvre, it provided yet another piece of missing context to the Holocaust. Eventually, the novella was seen as his lost jewel. French, Spanish, and Italian translations appeared. Students found it required reading. In 1984, the director Alex Corti made it into a prize-winning film for Austrian and Italian television. It too is a departure from Werfel and it strangely lacks his black comedy and literary justice in the end.

This new translation is a latecomer to the rediscovery, and even though it sets the clock back seventy years, readers should not feel too far removed from the present. Werfel's Austria in 1936 should remind us in some ways of the present. Austria was divided then between the Socialists in the cities and the Patriotic Front in what could be called its red states. Bureaucrats, then as now, were in charge of what continuity and stability existed. And Austria, like us, had this lingering sense of greatness and purpose. The novella's many motifs, woven into its economy of form, seem uncomfortably close – body consciousness, the anxiety of aging, of having no children, the male biological clock, and so on. Similarities between that time and ours aside, what comes next is complete in English, a reading experience that, in the choice of words and style, is played on a "period instrument," in tune with Werfel's imagination, his psyche, and his Vienna, a side of Austria you don't see in *The Sound of Music* and *The Third Man*.

JAMES REIDEL

PALE BLUE INK IN A LADY'S HAND

April in October

The morning mail lay on the breakfast table. It was a substantial batch of letters because Leonidas had just celebrated his fiftieth birthday and stragglers were still coming in wishing him well. Leonidas was really named Leonidas. For a first name that was as much burdensome as it was heroic, he could thank his father, an impoverished high school teacher who had also left him a full set of Greek and Roman classics and a ten-year run of *Tübingen Studies in Ancient Philology*. Fortunately the gravity of Leonidas could be condensed to plain Leo. His friends called him that and Amelie had never called him anything but Leon. She did so now with her dusky voice, melodiously accenting and drawing out the note on the second syllable.

"You are unbearably popular, León," she said. "Twelve more congratulation letters at least . . ."

Leonidas smiled at his wife as though he needed to be embarrassed and apologetic for having turned fifty and reaching the top of his brilliant career all at once. For some months now he was the section chief at the Ministry of Culture and Education and counted among the forty or so government bureaucrats who really ran the country. His composed, white hand absentmindedly toyed with the thick pile of letters.

Amelie carefully spooned out a grapefruit. That was all she had to eat in the morning. Her bathrobe had slid from her shoulders. She wore a black leotard in which she ritually performed her daily gymnastics. The glass door on the terrace was open halfway. It was rather warm for the season. From his place Leonidas could see beyond their terrace that sea of gardens that was the western suburbs of Vienna – all the way to the mountains on whose slopes the metropolis ebbed. With a glance he scrutinized the weather, which played an important role in his capacity for leisure and work. Today the world presented itself as a mild October day with a kind of strained, capricious youthfulness that more resembled a day in April. Over the expanse of vineyards that formed the Hietzing district's border, thick, fast-moving clouds scudded snow white with sharply delineated edges. Where the sky opened, it featured a naked and, for this time of year, nearly shameless spring blue. The garden, which had hardly changed color, retained that leathery persistence of summer. Light breezes, as mischievous as little street Arabs, blew from different directions with the leaves, which still clung fast to their branches.

Rather beautiful, thought Leonidas, I think I shall walk to work. And he smiled again. But it was a strange, mixed smile, dashing and mocking at the same time. Whenever Leonidas felt consciously pleased with himself, he smiled – dashing and mocking. Like so many handsome, healthy men in fine form, men who had risen to a high position in life, he tended to feel an exceptional well-being during the first hours of the morning. Out of that nonentity of night one virtually cruised everyday across this bridge, a newborn astonishment that is fully conscious of one's success in life. And this success could only be seen as the real thing: son of a poor, eighth-grade high school teacher. A nobody, without family, without name, even worse, saddled with a puffed-up first name. What a cold, depressing time it was – those student years. One had to slog through it with the help of stipends and by tutoring rich, fat, and stupid boys. That was hard, mastering the hunger blinking out of your own eyes when your slow students were being called to the table. But a suit still hung in an empty closet. A perfectly new suit that needed only a few alterations. This tuxedo had been inherited. A study partner, his boardinghouse neighbor, had left it to Leonidas in his will, after which he, without giving any notice, blew his brains out in the adjoining room. It had happened as though in a fairytale, for such formal attire is make-or-break in a university student's life. The owner of the suit was an "intellectual Israelite." (This is what the guarded and delicately strung Leonidas, who abhorred such open expressions of painful reality, thought of his benefactor.) But back then, those people were so incredibly well-off that they could easily afford such a luxurious motive for suicide as world-weariness.

That suit – whoever possesses one can go to balls and other social events. He who looks good in a tailcoat and has a certain talent for dancing the way Leonidas did, can make people like him fast, make friends, become acquainted with radiant young ladies, get invited into the "best homes." At least that's the way it was in that magic world in which there was social rank – and therein was the Unattainable, which awaited the chosen winner so long as he reached for it. The career of the poor home tutor began by sheer chance when Leonidas was given a ticket to one of the big cotillions.

Thereby the providence of the suicide's suit paid off. That desperate author of his last will and testament had laid down his life, helping his far luckier beneficiary across the threshold into a shining future. And this Leonidas, in the ever-tightening Thermopylæ of his youth, in no way stood down to the supremacy of an arrogant society. Not only Amelie, but other women too asserted there had never been such a dancer nor would there ever be again. It must be said that León's domain was the waltz, and who but he danced to the left as on air, tenderly, at once inescapably firm and relaxed? In the lively two-step of that strange epoch he proved to be a master romantic, a leader of women (in Leon's opinion) when the modern, popular dances of the masses in their dull, apathetic crowds afforded only this mechanical, confining routine of uninspired limbs trotting about.

Even when Leonidas reminded himself of his faded triumphs as a dancer, that characteristically mixed smile played across his handsome mouth with flashing teeth and a delicate, pencil-thin mustache that was still blond. Several times a day he considered himself to be an utter darling of the gods. If one were to question his "world view," he would openly admit that he regarded the universe as a venue whose sole intent and purpose was to pamper those divinely favored like him, from the bottom to the top, and to furnish them with power, honor, splendor and luxury. Wasn't his own life absolute proof of this charitable disposition of the world? It took just one bullet in the room next to his shabby student's digs to inherit a practically brand-new tuxedo. And from there on his life was a song. He attended a few balls during the carnival season. He danced gloriously without ever having taken a lesson. Then it rained invitations. Within a year he belonged to the young set and swept them off their feet. Whenever his all too classical name came up, a smiling regard informed every face. It wasn't easy to come by the working capital for such a popular double life. He succeeded with his diligence, his perseverance, his unassumingness. Before long he passed every one of his exams. Glowing recommendations opened doors to the civil service. He soon experienced the prompt favor of his superiors, who could not praise his self-effacing charm high enough. There followed, after only a few years, a much-envied promotion to the central authority, usually set aside for those stellar names, the most handpicked among the children of privilege. And then this wild infatuation of the eighteen-year-old Amelie Paradini, the image of beauty . . .

Each morning he woke up to this same wondrous serenity and not without justification. *Paradini* – one made no mistake if he or she paid attention to this name. Indeed, it was the world-famous House of Paradini (with branches in every major city). Of course, their equity has since been absorbed by the major banks. But twenty years ago Amelie was the richest heiress in the city. And not one of the glittering names from the aristocracy and the industrialists, not one of those nose-in-the-air suitors conquered the pretty young thing save he, the son of a starving Latin teacher, a young man with the pendulous name of Leonidas who owned nothing more than a well-fitting if macabre suit. But the word "conquered" would be a mistake for apparently he was, in this love story, not the hunter but rather the hunted. With unyielding energy the young girl pushed their marriage through despite the bitter resistance of her entire millionaire clan.

7

Now here she sits opposite him, like any other morning, Amelie, his life's great – his greatest achievement. Curiously, the essentials of their relationship have not changed. He still feels like the courted, the conceder, the giver, despite her wealth that surrounds him at every turn like the air, warm and comfortable. Incidentally, as Leonidas had pointed out, not without being impeccably precise, he did not regard Amelie's property as his in any way. From the very beginning he erected a sound wall between this very disproportionate "mine" and "yours." He regarded himself in this lavish and far too roomy mansion for two people as a tenant, a renter, as a paying guest, dedicating his entire salary as a civil servant without deduction for the common upkeep. From the very first day of their marriage he had insisted on this distinction. Knowing smiles might have been exchanged among society, but Amelie was charmed by the manly pride of her beloved, her chosen one. He had just reached the high point of life and stood poised to slowly descend its stairs. At fifty he had a thirty-eight or -nine-year-old wife who, in his eyes, still looked dazzling.

In the demure, revealing October light, Amelie's bare shoulders and arms were immaculate, not one blemish, not one tiny hair. The perfumed, marble white skin came not only from good breeding, it came from constant cosmetic care, which she took as seriously as a divine duty. Amelie wanted to remain young and beautiful and thin for Leonidas. Thin above all else. That required that she be hard on herself. She strayed not from the sheer path of this virtue. Her small breasts showed pointed and firm under her black leotard. They were the breasts of an eighteen-year-old.

We pay for those virgin breasts with childlessness, the husband thinks now. And this notion took him by surprise

8

for as the determined defender of his undivided pleasure he had never entertained a desire for children. For a second he plunged into that look in Amelie's eyes. They are green and clear today. Leonidas knew this fickle and ominous color well for on certain days his wife had eyes that changed with the weather. "April eyes," he had called them once. And at such times one had to be careful. Scenes lie in the air without the least provocation. Oddly enough those eyes are the only thing that run counter to Amelie still the teenage girl. They are older than her. Her eye pencil makes them look rigid. Shadows and a tired bluish cast circles them with the first hints of decline. So it is in the cleanest of rooms that deposits of dust and soot collect in certain places. Something already seemed ravaged in that female face, which now held him fast.

Leonidas turned away. Then Amelie said, "When are you going to finally open your mail?"

"It's such a bore," he murmured, looking somewhat surprised by the pile of letters on which his hand still rested reluctantly, hesitant. Then he spread out almost a dozen before him like a card player and looked them over in that routine way of the civil servant, the kind who can grasp the meaning of their "priority" with half a glance. There were eleven letters. Ten of them were addressed by a typewriter. The eleventh in that monotonous row stood out all the more for its handwriting in pale blue ink. The liberal strokes of a woman, rapid, a little too constricted. Leonidas instinctively lowered his head for he had become deathly pale. He needed a few seconds to collect himself. His hands were frostbitten with what came next. Amelie will now ask about this pale blue handwriting. But Amelie asked nothing. She was looking attentively at the newspaper that lay next to her place setting like someone who did not without

9

willpower feel obligated very much to keep up with the daily menace of contemporary events. Leonidas said something so as to say anything. He choked on the unnaturalness of his tone:

"Right you are . . . nothing but dreary congratulations . . ." Then he shuffled the letters back into a pile – once more with the hands of a card shark – and put them with exemplary casualness into his breast pocket. His hands behaved with more honesty than his voice. Amelie did not look up from the newspaper as she spoke:

"If it's alright with you, I could answer all this terrible rubbish for you, León . . ."

Leonidas, however, had already gotten up, having mastered himself. He smoothed out his gray flannel coat, pulled the cuffs from the sleeves, placed his hands on his slim waist and balanced several times on the tips of his toes as though he could prove and savor the suppleness of his superbly developed form this way:

"You are much too good, my dear, to be my secretary," he smiled elatedly sardonic. "My young people will take care of that in no time at all. Hopefully your day is not empty. And please don't forget we're going to the opera this evening . . ."

He leaned over and gave her hair a kiss of elaborate intimacy. She gave him a long look, with those eyes that were older than herself.

His narrow face was pink and freshly, and wonderfully, shaved. It radiated with smoothness, with that indestructible smoothness that both troubled and held her spellbound from the beginning.

SECOND CHAPTER

The Recurrence of the Same

After Leonidas had said good-bye to Amelie, he did not leave the house right away. The letter in the pale blue handwriting burned too much in his pocket. He tended not to read letters or newspapers on the street. Strictly speaking, it did not befit a man of his rank and reputation. On the other hand, he did not have the clear conscience and patience to wait long enough until he would be undisturbed in his big office at the ministry. So he did what he had so often done as a boy when he had a secret to hide, a dirty picture to look at, a forbidden book to read. No different than a boy of fifteen, the fifty-year-old, taking care that no one saw him, looked nervously in every direction and then locked himself inside the most secluded room in the house.

For a long time he stared with terrified eyes at that severe, stilted woman's cursive, weighing the limp envelope incessantly in his hand, not daring to open it. With ever more personal expression, the economy of every letter looked on and gradually filled his entire being like a poison dart, paralyzing his heart with every beat. That he would ever have to face Vera's handwriting again, even in a cruel nightmare, he had considered impossible. What had incomprehensibly

11

– unworthily – frightened him just now when he stared at her letter among his unimportant mail? It was an utter terror from the very beginning of his life. But a man who had reached the top and nearly completed his orbit should not be afraid. Luckily Amelie had not noticed. Why this fear that still tingled in every limb? But it's old history, stupid, banal, a youthful fling, twenty times beyond the statute of limitations. He had really more on his conscience than the matter with Vera. As an important civil servant, he was forced fairly often to make decisions affecting people's fates, needful, painful decisions. In his position one had to be a little like God. You create these fates. You shelve them – *ad acta*. They wander from the desk of life into dead files. With time, thank God, everything dissolves uncomplainingly into nothingness. Thus Vera too seemed to have already disappeared, uncomplaining, into a void . . .

It had to have been at least fifteen years ago when he had last held a letter from Vera in his hand as he did now, in a similar situation, and in a no less miserable toilet. Back then Amelie's jealousy knew no bounds and her emotional distrust could always smell something. The only thing he could do was destroy the letter. *Back then*. Destroying it unread, that was something else indeed. It was dirty cowardice, piggishness par excellence. This time Leonidas, that darling of the gods, could do nothing to deceive himself. I tore up the last letter unread – and I will tear up today's as well – to know nothing. He who knows nothing can't be involved. What I didn't need to know fifteen years ago, I need to know even a hundred times less now. That's that, filed away. I consider it common law, without qualification, that there's nothing here anymore. It's outrageous of this woman to once more make me see she exists so up close. How is she now, what does she look like?

Leonidas did not have the least idea what Vera looked like now. Worse, he did not know how she had looked back then, that time of the only real love in his life. Nor could he recall her eyes, nor the shimmer of her hair, nor her face, her form. The more he tried to conjure up her strange, lost image, the more hopeless the void that she had left behind in him, as though she intended to mock him. Vera, as it were, was the infuriating symptom of deficiency in his otherwise smoothly calligraphic and manicured memory. Why couldn't she just go to hell for once and stay what she had been for the past fifteen years, a nice, flat grave in a spot that no one can find anymore?

With unmistakable guile, this woman who withdrew her image from the faithless lover, materialized with her personality in those few words that addressed the envelope. They were full of a terrible presence, those fine, featherlike strokes. The section chief began to sweat. He held the letter in his hand like a criminal subpoena, no, like a court sentence. Then suddenly that July day fifteen years ago came back, bright and clear, down to its most fleeting details.

Summer! A glorious alpine vacation in St. Gilgen. Leonidas and Amelie were still practically young newlyweds. They stayed in a small hotel on the enchanting shore of the lake. They had arranged a leisurely mountain climb for a party of friends. In a matter of minutes a little steamer, which takes hikers to the starting point, would dock by the hotel. The lobby of the guesthouse resembled an enormous farm kitchen. Through the windows, shaded with a lattice of wild grapevine, the sun reached only a little with thick drops of honey. The room itself was dark. But it was a darkness like a vacuum, one that curiously dazzles the eyes. Leonidas stepped up to the hotel desk and asked the porter for his mail. There were three letters and among them this one with the pressed, perpendicular handwriting of a woman in light blue ink. Then Leonidas felt Amelie standing behind him, familiarly putting a hand on his shoulder. She asked if anything had come for her. He didn't know how he pulled it off, like a magic trick, concealing Vera's letter in his breast pocket. The amber-hued gloom helped. Luckily the friends they were waiting for appeared. After some cheerful greetings Leonidas slipped away. He still had five minutes to read the letter. But he did not read it. Instead he turned it over and over again unopened. Vera had written after three years of dead silence. She had written to him after he had behaved more caddishly, more terribly than any man had ever been to a lover. First he told the most despicable of cowardly lies, for he was already married for three years, that he could not live without her. And then that cleverly faked farewell from the window of a railway car: "Take care, darling – in two weeks we'll be together!" With these words he simply disappeared, giving no more thought to the existence of Fraulein Vera Wormser. If she wrote him now, a creature like Vera, then behind it was a terrible test of her will. This letter was nothing but a distress call from someone in dire circumstances. The worst of it was that Vera had written the letter from here. She was in St. Gilgen. It was there in black and white on the back of the envelope. She was staying in a pension on the other side of the lake. Leonidas had already pulled out a penknife to slit open the envelope, his punctilio

14

as ridiculous as it was revealing. But he did not open the penknife. If he read the letter, if what he dared not imagine turned out certainly to be there, there was no going back. For several seconds he considered the possibility and prospect of confessing. What in heaven would make him go to his young wife, to Amelie Paradini, who loved him fanatically, who surprised the world by marrying him, and confess to this exquisite creature from out of the blue, without further delay, that he had already cheated on her after one year of marriage in the most calculated way? That would destroy his very existence and Amelie's life without ever helping Vera. He stood helpless in the bathroom stall as the seconds passed. His lack of character, his fear disgusted him. The weightless letter lay heavy in his hand. The paper of the envelope was thin and not lined. The writing inside vaguely came through. He tried to make it out this way and that – nothing. A bumblebee buzzed through the open transom and was caught there like him. Despair, sorrow, guilt filled him and suddenly he felt this violent anger toward Vera. But she had seemed to understand that it was all a mad lark that had only happened thanks to a coincidence and his lies. He had acted no differently than a god from antiquity who changes his form and bends down to a child of man. Therein was the nobility, the beauty to this whole thing. Vera appeared to be over it, of that he was certain. For whatever might have happened to her, in the three years since his disappearance she had not made herself known, not one line, not one word, not one personal message. Everything was over with and sorted out for the best. He gave her a lot of credit for this, for sensibly falling in line to the inevitable. And now this letter. Only a stroke of luck prevented it from falling into Amelie's hands. And not just the letter. She was here pursuing him, taking a dip in this mountain lake where the entire world gathered now in that horrible family month of July. With some irritation Leonidas thought, Vera is still just another "intellectual Israelite." No matter how far they come, something always trips these people up. Mostly it's tact, this fine art of not bothering your fellow man. Why, for example, did his friend and fellow student, who had left him that suitful of success, shoot himself at eight in the evening, at such a convivial hour, in the next room? Couldn't he have done that just as well elsewhere, at a time when Leonidas was not nearby? But no! Every act, even the most desperate, must be underlined and set in bitter quotation marks. Always too much or too little. Proof of that distinctive lack of discretion. It was unspeakably tactless of Vera to come to St. Gilgen in July when we want to spend two weeks of hard-earned vacation – she has to certainly realize that. Suppose he met her on that steamboat, what was he supposed to do? He knew naturally what to do – not to recognize her, not to say hello, to look right through her, heedlessly debonair, and make laughing conversation with Amelie and the rest of that small company without batting an eye. But how dear the cost of maintaining his dignity while being so perfectly scandalous. It would cost him his steel nerves and self-confidence for an entire week of his all-too-short vacation. He had no appetite for that. The next days were ruined. And he must quickly come up with a plausible reason for Amelie, by tomorrow afternoon at the latest, to cut short their stay in charming St. Gilgen. But wherever they went, whether it was the Tyrol, the Lido, or the North Sea, the possibility would follow him everywhere, the one he dared not think through to the end. The rapid descent of these considerations caused him to forget about the letter in his hand. A curiosity had suddenly seized him now. He wanted to know how she was doing. Maybe these gloomy notions and fears were just figments of his easily excitable hypochondria. Maybe he'd be breathing a sigh of relief if he read the letter. The fat summer bee, his cellmate, finally found a gap in the window and droned outside to freedom. All at once it was terribly still in this miserable corner. Leonidas opened the penknife to slit the letter. The ancient little steamer, small and decrepit, tooted, a child's toy of a forgotten era. The paddlewheel could be heard churning up the water. After a brief stillness, the shadow pattern of the grape leaves began to play upon the wall again. Time's up. Amelie will already be nervously calling: León. His heart pounded as he tore the letter into little pieces and made them go away . . .

Eternal recurrence of the same – that such a thing really existed astonished Leonidas. Vera's letter of today had placed him in the same shameful position as fifteen years ago. It was the starting point of his sin against Vera and Amelie. Everything agreed down to the smallest hair. Getting the mail in the presence of his wife at the same time as today. Now he read the return address on the back of the envelope: "Dr. Vera Wormser, c/o." Then followed the name of the Park Hotel, which was in the next neighborhood, two streets over. Vera had come now as then to look for him, to corner him. But instead of a summer bumblebee, some ancient autumn flies hummed asthmatically while sharing in his captivity. Leonidas heard himself, not without surprise, chuckle to himself. This fear from before, the heart skipping a beat, was not only beneath him but also silly. Couldn't he have calmly torn up the letter, read or unread, in front of Amelie? An annoyance, a public petition, like a hundred others, nothing more. Fifteen years, no, fifteen plus three years! That made it sound simple. But eighteen years are a metamorphosis ad infinitum. They add up to more than half a generation, nearly enough to replace the living, an ocean of time that would water down any other crime to nothing more than cowardly bad manners in love. What kind of a dishrag was he who could not wipe away this mummified history, who'd lost the beautiful serenity of his morning, he, a fifty-year-old at the height of his career? The whole curse he diagnosed as stemming from the half-breeding of his heart. One half was too softhearted, the other blew with the wind. Therefore, he had suffered throughout his life with a "depraved heart." This way of putting it, he felt, ran counter to good taste. But it perfectly expressed the way his soul felt a little indisposed. Wasn't this terrible sentimentalism over the pale blue feminine handwriting proof of a chivalrous nature, compassionate, full of scruples, one that cannot get over nor forgive oneself for a moral blunder practically from another time? Leonidas answered this question in the affirmative and without reservation. He had to congratulate himself, albeit with a dash of melancholy. He could see a handsome, seductive man, one who except for that passionate episode with Vera could only be blamed for nine, maybe as many as eleven gratuitous escapades outside of his marriage.

He took a deep breath and smiled. Now he wanted to bring Vera to an end for good. Fraulein Dr. Vera Wormser, Ph.D., Philosophy. Even in this calling there was that confrontational inclination, that superiority. (Miss Doctor? No, hopefully Madame Doctor. Married or widowed.) In the open little window was that sky of puffy clouds. Leonidas decided to tear up the letter. But the tear was hardly half an

18

inch before his hands stopped. Now the perfect opposite was happening from what happened at St. Gilgen fifteen years ago. He wanted to open the letter then, but tore it up. Now he wanted to tear it up, but opened it. From the injured sheet the concentrated personality of that lady's cursive in pale blue ink regarded him disdainfully as it expanded now into several lines.

The top of the letter had been dated in a rapid, precise stroke: "October seventh, 1936." One sees the lady mathematician, Leonidas disparaged. Amelie had never dated a letter in her entire life. And then he read: "To the esteemed Herr Section Chief." Good. There was nothing to object to in such a dry address. It was perfectly tactful, but there seemed to be a weak, even insuperable derision lingering behind it. No matter, there's nothing too intimate to fear in "To the esteemed Herr Section Chief." Let's read on.

"I have forced myself now to turn to you for a favor. It does not concern me, but rather a talented young man who cannot continue his high school education in Germany for reasons that are well known and who would like to complete his studies here in Vienna. From what I understand, the possibility and handling of such a transfer is your special area of expertise, dear sir. Since I know no one else in my formerly native city, I regard it as my obligation to enlist you in this matter that is of extreme importance to me. Should you be prepared to address my request, it would suffice if you just let me know through your office. The young man will meet with you at the desired time and give you the necessary information. With many thanks, Vera W."

Leonidas read the letter twice from beginning to end without looking up. Then he gingerly put it back in his pocket like something precious. He felt so tired and slack that he could not find the strength to unlock the door and leave his jail cell. How absurdly unnecessary his childish escape into that oppressive little bathroom now seemed. He did not have to hide this letter from Amelie scared to death. He could have let this letter lie out in the open or calmly handed it to her across the table. It was the most harmless letter in the world, the most deceitful. He received a hundred such written requests every month asking him for favors, for him to intercede on someone's behalf. And yet, in these spare, direct lines existed a distance, a cold, careful deliberation before which he felt himself morally shrivel away. Maybe one day, who knows, on Judgment Day, a similar, insidiously level-headed composition will surface that is only understood by the creditor and debtor, to the murderer and victim, but to all others looks like the trivial details of the case – and in this very guise that redoubles the terror for the one concerned. God knows what wild ideas and impulsivities a civil servant could surrender to in the broad October daylight. Where did Judgment Day suddenly come from in an otherwise clean conscience? Leonidas already knew the letter by heart. "It is your special area of expertise, dear sir." So it's "dear sir." "I regard it as my obligation to enlist you in this matter that is of extreme importance to me." The dry style of a petition. And yet a sentence of granite force, with the tender subtlety of a spider web for the knowing, the guilty. "The young man will meet with you at the desired time and give you the necessary information." Necessary information. These two words tore open the abyss by concealing it. No state prosecutor, no crown jurist would be ashamed of such merciless ambiguity.

Leonidas was dumbstruck. After an eternity of eighteen years the truth had caught up with him at last. There was no way out, no retreat. He could no longer extricate himself from the truth that he had let happen in a minute of weakness. Now his world would change from the ground up and he with it. The ramifications of this metamorphosis were unforeseeable, this he knew, even if he was unable to understand them in his troubled mind.

A harmless request letter. But in this harmless request Vera had informed him that she had a grown son and that this son was his.

THIRD CHAPTER

High Court

Although time had passed, Leonidas walked much slower than usual along the boulevard through Hietzing. He supported himself on his umbrella as he strolled thoughtfully, but nevertheless kept an eye out so as not to miss exchanging a greeting. Often enough he had to "doff the melon," that is, his bowler, when the civil service pensioners and little burghers of this respectable, conservative part of town paid him a jolly compliment. He carried his coat over his arm for it had unexpectedly become warmer.

In that little while since Vera's letter had so radically changed his life, the weather of this October day changed too. Everywhere the sky had become overcast and those shamelessly naked areas showed no more. The clouds no longer sailed by as puffs of perfectly rendered steam. Now they hovered low with the color of dusty furniture covers. A dead calm made of thick flannel hung all about. The throbbing of motors, the crackle of trolley wires, the street noise near and far sounded upholstered. Every sound was both vociferous and indistinct as though it were telling to the world the history of these times with a full mouth. It was an unnaturally warm, dodgy kind of weather, the kind that inspired a fear of sudden death in older people. It could go any which way: thunderstorm and hail, a miserable steady rain, or a lazy peace treaty with the fall sun. From the bottom of his heart Leonidas hated this weather, which made it hard to breathe and seemed directly aimed at his state of mind.

The worst thing about the still air was that it prevented the section chief from thinking logically and making decisions, as though his academically trained mind could not work as freely and unfettered as usual, but rather in a thick, uncomfortable wool glove that did not let him take hold and grasp the rapidly increasing issues.

Vera had brought him down today after a silent, eighteen-year-old struggle, which had taken place outside of his life, so without really getting weaker. Her power alone had been to make him read the letter instead of tearing it up and thereby escaping the truth once more. Whether that was a mistake he had no way of knowing now. But it was a defeat no matter how you looked at it and, more importantly, a sudden switch in his life. For a quarter of an hour his life ran on new railroad tracks in an unknown direction. For now, fifteen minutes to be exact, he had a son. This son was about seventeen years old. The realization of being this unknown young man's father had not come unexpectedly and ambushed him out of thin air. In the twilight kingdom of his guilty conscience, Vera's child since the uncertain day of its birth lived a threatening, malevolently eerie existence in his anxiety and curiosity. Now, after an almost interminable incubation, in which his fear had nearly melted away, the ghost had suddenly taken on flesh and blood. That innocently malicious veiling of the truth in Vera's letter had in no way assuaged the helplessness of his confusion. Although he did not know the least thing about the character of his once beloved, he thought, nervously biting his lips, that this was the real Vera, this ruse of war. She is being vague. Is she being vague so as to compromise me? Or does she still allow me some hope? The letter obviously gives me the option of making my getaway. "Should you be prepared to address my request . . ." And when would I not be prepared? My God, that has to be it – with her vagueness she ties me in a double knot. I can no longer remain passive. By not writing the truth, she verifies it. And when it came to Vera the legal term "verifies" really did enter the section chief's mind.

In the middle of the crosswalk his good manners failed him. He stopped, exhaled a groan, took off his bowler, and dabbed at his brow. Two cars honked furiously. An indignant policeman directing traffic barked at him. Leonidas reached the opposite shore in forbidden leaps. It had occurred to him that his new son was very likely a Jewish boy. This was why he no longer could attend school in Germany. Living next to Germany was, at present, dangerous for everyone. Nobody knew how things would go in this country. It was an unequal battle. Any day the same laws could come down here. Even now any social contact between members of Vera's race and members of the government was, save for a few glitering exceptions, most impermissible. Those days were gone when he could inherit the tailcoat of an unfortunate colleague who had shot himself for no good reason other than he could no longer bear the idolized Richard Wagner's condemnation of his tribe. And now, at fifty, you suddenly had a child from this tribe. An incredible turn of events – the complications were inconceivable. Amelie?! But we aren't that far yet, Leonidas persuaded himself.

Again and again he tried very carefully "to compose" this defense in which he was both the guilty party and the victim. The well-trained official has the skill after all "to build a file" for any situation and thereby snatch it from that melting process of life. Leonidas, however, hardly succeeded in producing the same dry facts once more, let alone a wisp of those six weeks of burning love. Vera herself forbade it, just as she deprived him of her image. What remained was quite meager. Were he able, in these minutes of torment, to put himself before a court of law (before what court?), to paint a colorful picture of incriminating misconduct, it would be something like the following.

It happened during the thirteenth month of our marriage, your honor – so his matter-of-fact testimony would begin – for Amelie had received news that her maternal grandmother was gravely ill. This grandmother, an Englishwoman, was the most important personality in that snobby family of millionaires, the Paradinis. She idolized her youngest grand-daughter. Thus Amelie was forced to travel to Devonshire, the country seat of the dying woman, to defend a consider-able portion of her inheritance. Schemers and legacy hunters were at work. I considered it absolutely vital that my wife never move from that old woman's eyes in her final hours. Unfortunately, these final hours dragged on for three full months. I think I can say without making it up in hindsight that we, Amelie and I, were genuinely distressed by this first separation in our lives together. To be quite honest, how-ever, maybe I did feel a rather pleasant excitement all the same time at being on my own again. In the beginning of our relationship, Amelie was far more demanding, moody, easier to upset and make jealous than she is now, despite her once being madly in love, accustomed to the rhythms of my temperate lifestyle. Of course, she could easily play the Fairy Caprice. Her wealth made her mistress over me and that brutal status quo cannot be overturned despite one's culture, development, upbringing, and other such luxuries. In any case, we held a tearful, reluctant goodbye ceremony trackside at the West bahnhof. Meanwhile, my ministry had resolved to send me to Germany in order to learn at first hand about the exemplary organization of its university curricula. The arrangement and administration of universities, as you know, are my real specialty, my particular strength. In these areas I have accomplished much, something that cannot be easily eliminated from the history of education in my fatherland. For her part, Amelie was elated that I would be going to Heidelberg during our separation. She would have suffered very much if she had to leave me behind in that larger and more seductive setting of Vienna. The temptations of a charming German university town seemed to her as light as a feather. I even had to promise on my honor, so help me God, to leave Vienna on the day after her departure so as to immediately dedicate myself to my new assignment. To the second I honored my promise for I must confess that even now Amelie inspires a certain fear. I had no intention of rebelling against her superior position. She had her mind set on the subaltern clerk that I was then, whom she married against every objection, the extravagance of a pampered life for which every wish must be fulfilled. Who has theirs, will get theirs. Let there be no doubt, I am Amelie's property. The advantages of belonging to a stinking rich woman with a mind of her own and connected to a financially and socially influential family are very great. The disadvantages, however, are not a little large. Not even that strict separation of our estates, on which I always insisted, kept me from turning into a kind of kept man by dint of an intrinsic law of nature in that great fortune. First of all, if I were to lose Amelie, I would have positively more to lose than she would were she to lose me. (As an aside, I don't believe that Amelie could survive my loss.) These reasons made me insecure and anxious from day one. It required ceaseless self-control and foresight not to draw attention to my humiliating weaknesses while always remaining the consummately blithe husband who takes for granted his success with a careless shrug of his shoulders. – Twenty-four hours after our emotional farewell, I arrived in Heidelberg. In the lobby of the best hotel there I turned around. Suddenly that luxury, in which my marriage had placed me, disgusted me. It was as if I were homesick for that hardship and poverty of my student years. Then it occurred to me: Had I not been charged with studying lives and lifestyles of the students as well? So I rented a room in a cramped, cheap student hostel. And with the first meal at common table I saw Vera. I saw Vera Wormser again.

For everything that I now submit before the court, your honor, I have to ask that you bear with me. It is because I can't really remember the chain of events for which I am accused even though they sound, of course, very much like my infamous exploits. Therefore I have some vague idea of them the way someone knows he has read something somewhere a long time ago. He can barely summon it back. But it doesn't exist inside him like his own past. It is abstract and empty, a painfully embarrassing void before which he recoils from every attempt at reliving with any emotion. There is after all my lover, Miss Vera Wormser, a student of philosophy at the time. I recall that she was twenty-two years old when we were reunited in Heidelberg, nine years younger than me, three years older than Amelie. I recall that I had never seen a finer, more petite figure than Miss Wormser. Amelie is quite tall and slim. But she must struggle incessantly to be thin since nature has given her regal form a tendency to fill out. Without my ever making a single remark about it, Amelie instinctively understood that everything pompously female left me cold, that I feel an overwhelming fondness for the childlike, ethereal, translucent, touchingly tender, and fragile image of women, especially when it is paired with a bold, sensible mind. Amelie is dark blond. Vera has raven-black hair – parted in the middle and in stark contrast to her deep blue eyes. I report this because I know it, not because I see anything in front of me. I don't see Miss Wormser, who was my lover, with my inner eye. It's like someone carrying this conscious melody in his head without being able to hum it back. For years I could not imagine Vera of Heidelberg. Time and again another person inserted herself in between. This fourteen- or fifteen-year-old Vera, the way I, the threadbare student, saw her for the first time.

The Wormser family had once lived in Vienna. The father was a doctor much in demand. He was a small man with a delicate frame and a salt-and-pepper beard who spoke very little, who would unexpectedly bring a medical periodical or pamphlet to the dinner table and pore over it without looking up at anybody. In him I made my first acquaintance with the perfect "intellectual Israelite" given his reverence for printed paper, with his deep faith in open-minded inquiry, which in these people replaces natural instincts and self-control. How impressed I was at the time by that impatient intensity, which allowed no accepted truth without an argument. I felt confused, like nothing before his scalpel-like acuity. He had already been a widower for some time and painted over the mournful primer of his features was an inextinguishably ironic smile. An older lady, who also served as the office nurse, ran the household. Doctor Wormser, some said, was a physician who towered over many of the leading lights of the university faculty in science and in the accuracy of his diagnoses. I had been recommended to this home to prepare the seventeen-year-old Jacques, Vera's brother, for his exams. Jacques had missed several months of school due to a lengthy illness and now his deficiencies had to be overcome in a hurry. He was a pale, sleepy-looking boy who held me in contempt and often tormented me mercilessly with his absentmindedness, his being oppositional (now I know why). He volunteered in the first weeks of the war and later fell at Rava Ruska.

How happy I was, nevertheless, during the hardest period of my life, to have found a home tutoring position for such a long engagement. I had no future. That a semester later I would succeed in making that leap from my dull underworld into the light of the world above, and with the animated personality to go with it, was as yet undreamable. I already thought I had drawn the winning ticket at the Wormser house because, without it being stipulated, I was fed lunch daily. The doctor usually came home around that time while Jacques and I were still sitting there over his textbooks. He would call us to the table, whereby he would often parody my unfortunate first name after that famous inscription on the ancient tomb of Leonidas and his heroes:

> *Traveler, if you go to Sparta,*
> *proclaim in that place,*
> *You saw us here as commanded,*
> *feeding our face.*

It was the lightest of jests, but it put me to shame and hurt every time. Lunchtime at the Wormsers became a customary rite for me. Vera typically arrived late. She was a high school student like her brother. But her school was in another district. She had a long walk home. She wore her hair long back then. It fell upon her delicate shoulders. Her features looked carved from moonstone and were dominated by these large eyes whose maddening blue seemed, from this cold detachment, to be lost in deep shadows under dark brows and lashes. I seldom met those eyes, which had the most arrogant, the most disdainful look from a girl that I ever had to endure. I was her brother's home tutor, just an insignificant student with a pimply face, pale as cheese, and burning eyes all the time – a meaningless void, insecurity incarnate. I do not exaggerate. Until this implausible turning point in my life, I was without a doubt an unhandsome, awkward fellow who felt despised by everyone and especially by every woman. To a certain extent I had reached the "depth" of my existence. No one would have paid a penny for lessons from this shabby student. I wouldn't. I had exhausted all self-confidence. How should I know that during these disastrous months I would soon be infinitely surprised at myself? (Everything happened then as though without my help.) In my misery at twenty-three, I was not even a fully evolved lemur. Yet Vera, although a child, seemed far more mature in age and far more secure. Whenever her eyes passed over me at the table, I stiffened under the arctic cold temperature of her indifference. Then I had this wish, to disappear into nothing so that Vera did not have to see the most unappetizing and unsympathetic man in the world with her beautiful eyes anymore.

Next to birth and death a person experiences a third catastrophic step on his earthly path. I would call it "social parturition" without being in total agreement with this somewhat too brilliant expression. I mean that convulsive transition from the totally egoless, invisible state of the young person to his first self-affirmation inside the framework of an established group. How many perish at this birth or get damaged for life. It is no mean achievement to be fifty years old and be honored and valued to boot. At twenty-three, a case overdue, I wanted to die every day, mostly when I sat at Dr. Wormser's family table. With my heart throbbing wildly I waited every time for Vera's pending entrance. When she appeared at the door, it was for me such terrible bliss that I nearly choked. She kissed her father on the forehead, gave her brother a pat, and absentmindedly extended her hand in my direction. Now and then she even addressed me.

It usually concerned questions pertaining to one of the topics that had come up in school that day. With a greedy voice I tried to answer them all and let my light shine forth. Vera always knew how to ask in such a way that I was taking the test, and she giving it, because she by no means had any need of me, this unfailing fount of knowledge, which is how I fancied myself. She accepted nothing as bona fide. In this way she was her father's daughter. If she suddenly cut off my vain sermon – her eyes seeing right past me – with an adamant "Why is that?" her genius for skepticism would fluster me to the point of speechlessness. I myself never asked "Why?" having not the slightest doubt in the final say of every scholar. I was not the son of a schoolman, who regarded memorization as the best method of teaching, for nothing. Vera also set traps for me sometimes and, in my eagerness, I fell into them. It was then that Dr. Wormser smiled wearily from irony or ironically from weariness, who could tell with him. Vera's intelligence, her critical sense, her unerringness were only exceeded by the unapproachable attraction of her appearance that took my breath away again and again. I loved the girl even more despairingly. I lived through several weeks of the most terrible sentimentality. At night I cried my pillow wet. I, who would call the most desirable beauty of Vienna mine a few years later, for a few weeks believed I would never be worthy of that hard schoolgirl Vera. I was drunk to death with hopelessness. Two character traits of the adored one hurled me into the abyss of my unworthiness: the purity of her mind and something sweetly foreign that brought me to the edge of shuddering with ecstasy. My lone victory was that I did not let on. I hardly looked at Vera and made an effort to wear a fixed, nonchalant expression. As it goes for those walking disasters in love, so it was for me. Again and again I would slip up or do something clumsy that made me the laughingstock. I knocked to the floor a piece of Venetian glass that Vera especially loved. When I spilled red wine across a clean tablecloth, I refused to eat out of pure embarrassment and stupid pride. I stood up as hungry as I had sat down without any hope of supper. It was a senseless but heroic renunciation that did not impress Vera in the least. Once I bought – I could not pay the rent for my room because of them – the most beautiful long-stemmed roses. But I lost the courage to give them to Vera and hid them instead behind a closet in the outer hall where they wilted in shame. I soon became like the shy lover in some old-fashioned farce, just more futile and annoying. Another time, when we were already sitting for dessert, I sensed how my all-too-tight pants had split open in the middle of the most alarming place. My coat did not reach down to cover the spot. How was I to rescue my self-confidence, God in heaven, without exposing myself to Vera? Never before or after was there ever such a hell as these minutes.

You can see, your honor, how fluid my memory is when I apply it to the Wormser house and the period of my first, and last, unfortunate love. I find nothing objectionable in the court's advice: Defendant, keep to the facts. We're not psychiatrists, but rather a court. Why bother us with the emotional torment of a youth who, in very belated fashion, still had not overcome the lingering effects of sexual maturity? You pretty much discarded your timidity sooner rather than later, which you'll admit. When you inherited the suicide's suit, and saw in the mirror that it did you well, made you a proper-looking young man, you became all at once a changed man, that is, you became yourself. So whom do you want to impress with these boring stories? Do you see something in the puppy love that you've put on display as an excuse for your subsequent behavior? – I make no excuse, your honor. – It has been determined that you never revealed your feelings to the fourteen- or fifteen-year-old during your employment in the Wormser home. – My face never gave me away. – Defendant, please continue. You rented a room in Heidelberg, in a boardinghouse for students. There you met your victim again. – Yes, sir, I rented myself into that small boardinghouse and met Vera Wormser fully seven years since that first meal. After Jacques passed his exams thanks to my help, the family relocated to Germany. Someone had offered Wormser the directorship of a private hospital in Frankfurt and he took the job. But when I met Vera again, her father and brother were no longer alive. She was utterly alone in the world, saying, however, that she felt free and independent rather than alone. As coincidence would have it, I took my place by her at the long table . . .

I must interrupt myself, your honor, for even I have to
notice the hem-hawing and wooden quality of my recitation.
The more embarrassing my testimony becomes, the more I
need to collect myself for I am getting closer to that taboo,
this forbidden zone in my memory. There was, for example,
that same kind of heated exchange that had once flared up
at the first meal. I remember we disputed every kind of
intellectual topic that happened to be in fashion then. I
remember Vera being my most passionate opponent. But
despite my usually reliable memory, I no longer have any
memory of what we argued about. I guess I defended the
conventional position, securing the approval of the major-
ity, against Vera's devastating critique. But this time I really
didn't suffer defeat like I did before at the good doctor's
family table. I was thirty-one, impeccably dressed, an emis-
sary of the ministry. That day I had been seen in the company of his excellency, the university chancellor. I had money
to burn. Thus I existed, both inwardly and outwardly, in a
state of incredible superiority over all these young people to
whom Vera belonged as well. I had learned a great deal during the intervening years. I had acquired from my superiors
this bearing with its engagingly debonair entitlement and
authority, which is such a distinctive feature of our vener-
able tradition of Austrian officialdom. I knew how to talk.
Even more, I knew how to talk with such self-confidence
that everyone else fell silent. I was coming into contact with
many very important people then whose views and opin-
ions I now casually put forward as my own. I not only knew
the elite, I had become a part of it. Before his "social birth,"
the bourgeois young man overestimates the difficulty of
leaping into the world. I myself, for example, owed my aston-
ishing career not to any phenomenal attributes but rather to

three musical talents: a fine ear for human vanity, my sense of tact, and – most important of the three – this most adaptable skill at mimicry whose roots lie in the weakness of my character. How else did I, without even a premonition of the two-step, become one of the most popular waltzers of my day? As a big man, the pathetic home tutor now approached her, the once adored. I really do believe that Vera, after some initial disapproval, regarded me with ever more astonished, ever wider and bluer eyes. And did my old infatuation wake up with a bang? I don't just think, I know. I had since learned the game people play, man and woman. It was not just a wicked game, it was a mad compulsion, step by step, toward guilt that had been fixed from the beginning. I seem to recall that I kept myself under control rather well, that I showed nothing of my arousal, not out of miserable pride as before, but rather out of a delightful sense of purpose. Every day I considered exactly how I might show off my elegant appearance and mind to their best advantage. But something more than my contrived little attentions won over Vera. I intimated to her that I, at heart, shared in her carelessly radical views and that only my high position and reasons of state forced me to walk a "middle line." I think I turned red with joy for she was sure she had cured me of my "lies of convention." So I waited carefully for the right moment, that moment when the feeling is right. It happened faster than I dared to hope. It was on that fourth or fifth day of my stay that Vera gave herself to me. Her face I don't see, but I feel her tense surprise, which filled her before she became completely and utterly mine. I don't see where it took place. Everything's dark. Was it a room? Were there branches swaying under a night sky? I see nothing but the feeling of the beautiful moment I carry within me. There was nothing of Amelie's domineering intensity. It was lockjawed fear at first, then came this exhaled relaxation of her soft mouth, the dreamy acquiescence of her childlike limbs that I held in my arms, later a timid effort to be close, a tender trustfulness, an abundance of faith. No one was so unconditionally, so naively trusting as this sharp critic. Contrary to Vera's frank talk and boyish uninhibitedness, I could see in these moments that I was her first. As yet I didn't know that virginity, shielded from pitilessness and sport, is something holy . . .

I must stop here, your honor. Every step further ensnares me in a jungle. Even though I had knowingly and with arrant premeditation entered it back then, I can no longer find the entrance now. Yes, our love was a kind of jungle. Where did I go with my lover during this time? In how many gabled little towns and villages between the Taunus Mountains, in the Black Forest, in the Rhineland, in how many wine gardens, beer gardens, small hotels, and high-ceilinged rooms? I've lost track. It's all a blank. It doesn't get to the court's question. Somebody here asked: Do you plead guilty? I plead guilty. But my guilt does not lie in the simple fact of seduction. I took a girl ready to be taken. My guilt was that I turned her into my woman so utterly in bad faith like no other woman, not even Amelie. Those six lost weeks with Vera add up to the only real marriage in my life. And in that enormous skeptic I had implanted this enormous faith in myself only to let it be disgraced. That's my crime. Please, excuse me, I see that the court doesn't appreciate such a high tone. Yes, I acted like an operetta cavalier, a gigolo, like a totally typical marriage swindler. It began with all the class of that most trivial of all gestures. I hid my wedding ring. Out of necessity the first lie gave rise to the second and then the hundred that followed. But now comes the special flavor of my guilt. All those lies and the absolute trust of the deceived party intensified my lust in an inconceivable way. I planned our future together for Vera with this insistent eagerness. Smoothly, thoroughly, I provided for our domestic arrangements, which thrilled her. My plans left nothing out, not the layout, not the furnishing for our future dwelling, not the choice of the city district best situated to our advantage, not the choice of people whom I deemed worthy enough to associate with her – among them, of course, the most potent minds, the most aloof malcontents. My imagination outdid itself. Nothing had been left out of consideration. I sketched out the daily timetable of our happily married life together down to the smallest detail. Vera would interrupt her studies in Heidelberg and continue them in Vienna at my side. In Frankfurt we went into the most beautiful stores. I began to buy things for our house, and just to heighten my rapture I acquired every kind of intimate and immediate thing for a life together. I showered her with gifts so as to make her believe all the more. Despite her wild protests, I assembled an entire trousseau. This one time in my life that I was extravagant. When my money ran out, I wired for more. The entire day, like a fanatic, I wallowed in damask, silk, linen, lace, in mountains of sheer ladies' hosiery. How indescribably titillating it was when Vera's icy intelligence melted away and this smitten little female emerged in her utterly beautiful strangeness and with the unconditional devotion to her man that is such a distinguishing mark of this tribe. I do not see her, your honor, but I feel like we are going through the streets hand in hand, fingers interwoven. Oh, those cool, delicate fingers, how I sense them! I feel the melody of her steps in harmony next to mine. I had experienced nothing so beautiful as this hand in hand, this step by step. Yet while I fully experienced this, I enjoyed at the same time with a deep shudder this murder I was prepared to commit on the couple we made. And then came a day of parting. For Vera it was a joyous departure, for after a short separation I would make her mine forever. I see her face beneath the window of my railway carriage. She must have smiled up at me, with this abundance of calm trust. "Take care, my darling," I said. "I'll be back for you in two weeks." But when I sat alone in my compartment, I collapsed after all those weeks of tension and fell into this narcotic sleep. I slept for hours unawakenable and neglected to change trains at a large station. After a senseless trip I arrived at night in a city named Apolda. I remember that. I no longer can see Vera anymore, but I see clearly the sad railroad station bar, where I had to wait until the morning . . .

This is what Leonidas might have said. This is what he could have explained coherently before any court. He had available to him, was conscious of every little chip of stone in this mosaic. His feelings of love and guilt were there, but the scenes and images escaped him when he tried to reach for them. And above all, he could not escape the sensation of being put on trial unexpectedly. The weather, however, this terrible calm, in whose eye he saw himself while walking through the streets, defeated every attempt at "getting the story right" each time. He sensed his thoughts growing duller, ever more relaxing their grip. Was it not high time to make a decision? Had not the high court, with such bureaucratic tenacity, somewhere inside him and outside him, reached a verdict already? "Restitution to the child," read Article 1 of this judgment. And with more severity fell Article 2: "Restoration of the truth." But if he let himself tell Amelie the truth, this truth would destroy his marriage forever. Despite the passage of eighteen years, a creature such as Amelie could neither forgive nor get over his deceit and, worse, his lifelong lie. During these minutes he clung to his wife more than ever. He became weak. Why hadn't he torn up Vera's damned letter?

Leonidas raised his eyes. He went past the terrace side of the Hietzing Park Hotel where Fraulein Dr. Wormser stayed. The stacked balconies, overgrown with wild grapevines in their hundred shades of red, offered a friendly welcome. It must be charming to stay there now in October. The windows looked out onto Schönbrunn Park with the zoo on the right and, on the left, the so-called "Cavalier House" of the former imperial palace. He stopped in his tracks before the hotel entrance. It was about ten o'clock. Really not the hour at which a well-bred man might pay a call on a woman virtually a stranger . . . Go inside. Let her know you're there. Improvise a solution without long deliberation. From the doorway stepped some department head who nodded respectfully to the section chief. For God's sakes, can no one slip inside any place without being caught?

Leonidas fled across into the palace park. It no longer mattered now that he was running uncharacteristically late today or that the Minister of Education himself might be asking about him. The path between walls of baroque-cut yews swept endlessly into a vague distance. Somewhere there in that misty emptiness hovered the "Gloriette," an astral body in physical form, the ghost of a triumphal gate for some jubilee that seemed to lead into the well-ordered heaven of the *ancien régime* without any connection to a disenchanted world. It reeked all about of every kind of faded glory, of all dust – and baby diapers. Long columns of baby buggies were being pushed past Leonidas. Mothers and nursemaids led three- and four-year-olds by the hand whose babbling, gurgling, whining coming and going filled the air. Leonidas saw that any baby in a stroller, with its clenched fists, pouty mouth, preoccupied in the deep sleep of childhood, looked alike, easily confused, one from the other.

After another hundred steps he collapsed on a bench. During this moment a beamlet of October sun worked its way through and sprinkled the lawn opposite like a pencil-thin rainshower. Perhaps he had given too much credence to the whole story. In the end Vera's young man was probably not his son. *Pater semper incertus* – father unknown – so said Roman law. Proving it was his son did not depend on Vera alone after all, but on him as well. This paternity could be denied before any court. Leonidas turned to look at his neighbor on the bench. This neighbor was a sleeping old gent. Actually, he was not an old gent, just an old man. His tattered derby and prehistoric standup collar indicated one of those victims of the times who had seen better days, as the compassionless cliché says. He could have been a butler, unemployed for years. His gnarled hands lay heavily on his shrunken thighs like reproaches. Never before had Leonidas seen someone sleep they way his neighbor did. His mouth was open a bit, revealing these forlorn gap teeth, yet he did not noticeably seem to be breathing. From everywhere the deep lines and folds in his wasted face converged concentrically toward his eyes. Here the bridle paths, the cart trails, all the little avenues of life slid downhill altogether and spread over an abandoned countryside. Nothing moved there. Where the eyes had turned upward, two shadowed sandpits formed into which everything came to an end. Compared to death, this sleep offered nothing that recommended itself, for it retained vestiges of something convulsive, anxious, of putting up an indescribably weak defense . . .

Leonidas sprang up to get back to the promenade. After a few steps, something tottered and murmured behind him.

"Pardon me, lord baron, if I may, I've had nothing to warm my body for three days . . ."

"How old are you?" the section chief asked the sleeper, whose eyes appeared to be two barren empty pits even when awake.

"Fifty-one, lord duke," lamented the old man as though revealing every bit of an inadmissible age that no longer reckoned as his legal one without corroboration. Leonidas tore a large bill from his wallet and handed it to the bum and didn't look back.

Fifty-one. He cross-examined himself as though he had met his double, his twin brother, the other path his life might have taken that he had missed by a hair's breadth. Fifty years ago someone had pushed the wrinkled sleeper and him as babies, one alike as the other, through the park. He was still the handsome Leon, spic and span, with his trim blond mustache, showered and shaved, the impeccable masculine image, fit and refreshed. On his smooth face, life's avenues were neither impeded nor empty, but provided a cheerful passage. Here all sorts of smiles sped hither and thither, the conviviality, the disdain, the moods good and bad, the lie in every remark. He never slept that fleeting, agonized sleep of the park bench, but rather that full, sound, regular sleep of security in his big French bed. What hand had plucked him, the Wormsers' tutor, this wretch with split pants, from the certain jaws of ruination, and shoved another candidate in his place? He no longer saw his fortune, his ascent as nothing other than his own personal merit, the interplay of certain talents. The face of this wreck who was the same age had exposed the abyss, the one intended for him no less than this other, spared because of the same unfathomable unfairness.

A black horror came over Leonidas. But in this horror a blurry, bright spot stood out. The bright spot grew. It grew into a realization, the likes of which had never before stolen up on this moderately religious man: *You have a child, that's no small thing.* Only by a child is someone hopelessly chained to the world, to that merciless chain of cause and effect. One is responsible. One passes not only life, but death, the lies, the pain, the guilt. Above all the guilt. Whether I acknowledge the young man or not, I cannot change the objective fact. I can avoid him. But I cannot escape him. "Something has to happen," Leonidas whispered lost in thought while an inexpressibly disturbing clarity filled him.

At the park gate he impatiently hailed a cab.

"Ministry of Education!"

As a bold resolution grew inside him, he stared as though blind into a day from which the clouds had lifted just a little.

FOURTH CHAPTER

Leonidas Delivers for His Son

As soon as Leonidas entered his office he was handed a message that Herr Minister expected him at 11:10 in the conference room known as the Red Salon. The section chief regarded the secretary who brought him this message with a look of resignation and gave no answer. After a brief, surprising pause, the younger official laid a presentation folder down on the desk with circumspect emphasis. It concerned a mandatory meeting – as he meant by the appropriate unassumingness – presumably on the filling of vacant chairs at the universities. In this folder the section chief found all the dossiers in proper order.

"Thank you very much, my good man," Leonidas said without giving the folder one look of appreciation. Hesitating, the secretary vanished. He had expected his boss to flip through the dossiers per usual in his presence, to ask certain questions and make annotations so as not to look unprepared during his presentation before the minister. Today, however, Leonidas didn't think to do this.

Like others among the highest state officials, the section chief had no real respect for ministers. Subject to political power plays, they changed while he and his colleagues remained. The ministers washed in and washed out according to their parties, swimmers mostly gasping for air, desperately grabbing the planks of power. They had no real notion of how to conduct business inside a labyrinth, no fine sense for the sacred rules of the bureaucratic end-in-itself. They were all too often dispensable simpletons who had learned nothing more than to exercise their vulgar voices at mass rallies and annoyingly intervened for their party comrades and family connections through the back door. Meanwhile Leonidas and those like him had learned their office like musicians learning counterpoint after years of continuous practice. He and his colleagues had a nervous, intuitive feeling for every nuance of management and decision making. The ministers (in their eyes) simply played the part of political jumping jacks. They might strut about being dictatorial given the fashion of the times. But they, the department heads, cast their irremovable shadows over these tyrants. No matter what party's dishwater flooded the bureaucracy, they held all the strings. One needed them. With Mandarin superiority, they kept to the background. They despised the public, the newspaper, the self-advertisements of those daily heroes – and Leonidas more than anyone else for he was rich and independent.

He pushed the folder away, sprang up, and began pacing back and forth with long strides in his spacious suite. What strengths rained down on his soul, from this room, which was all-business. This was his kingdom, not Amelie's luxurious house. The mighty desk with its distinguished emptiness, the red club chairs with their worn leather, the bookshelf that displayed his father's Greek and Roman classics and thick philological journals, God knew why, the filing cabinets, the high windows, the mantelpiece with the gilded,

Congress-period clock; on the walls, age-darkened portraits of various forgotten dukes and ministers: all of these tired things lacking in personality – from the Imperial Furniture Depot – were like props loaned to support his vacillating feelings. He took a deep breath of the room's poorly dusted dignity. His resolve was irrevocably calm. He would tell his wife the whole truth today. Yes, at dinner. It would be best during dessert or over black coffee. Like a politician preparing a speech, he listened to himself with an inner ear:

– If it's quite all right with you, dear, let's remain sitting for a moment. Don't be frightened, I have something that has been pressing on my heart for many years. Up until today I've just not had the courage. You know me, Amelie, I can put up with anything except catastrophes, emotional outbursts, scenes, I can't bear seeing you unhappy . . . I love you today as I have always loved you, and I have always loved you as I love you today. Our marriage is the sacred temple of my life, you know I really hate being so pathetic. I hope that, in my love, I have let myself be guilty of very little. What I mean is, there is one, very great transgression. It is up to you to punish me, to punish me very hard. I am prepared for anything, dearest Amelie, I will submit myself unconditionally to your judgment, I will also leave our, that is, your house if that is your command and find a modest place to live somewhere nearby. But before you decide, I beg you please consider that my sin took place at least eighteen years ago and that not one cell in our bodies, not one feeling in our souls is the same as it was then. I want nothing glossed over, but I know that during our unfortunate separation I never so much as cheated on you as I gave in to a devilish compulsion. Believe me. Isn't our long, happy marriage not living proof? You do realize that in five, six years,

45

it's up to you, we celebrate our silver anniversary? Unfortunately, however, my incomprehensible digression had consequences. There is a child, that is, a young man of seventeen. I first learned about it today. I swear to you. Please don't say anything irrational yet, Amelie, no rash decisions made in anger. I will leave the room. I will let you alone. So that you can think calmly. Whatever you decide to do about me, I will have to look after this young man. –

This is nothing. It's mushy, it's mewling. I've got to speak more sparingly, with a hard edge, be manlier, without beating around the bush and then ambushing her, not be so chicken-hearted, so having to beg, so sentimental. This old, putrid sentimentality keeps coming to the surface in me. Amelie won't believe it for a minute – the hardest she can punish me is by throwing me out and I have grown too soft, become too comfortable in my pampered state, so hopelessly dependent on her money. She may not, for God's sake, have any idea that I'd be lost without our house, our two cars, our staff, our fine cuisine, our conviviality, our travel, even though I really would be lost, in all likelihood, without this damnably pleasant but embarrassing situation.

Leonidas sought a new, leaner way to word his confession. But he failed once more. When he reached the fourth version, he suddenly slammed his fist down on the table. That damnable obsession of the bureaucrat, for everything a motivation, for everything a basis. Didn't real life reside in the unseen, in the spur of a moment? Had he, spoiled to death by his success and well-being, truly forgotten how to fend for himself at fifty? The secretary knocked. Eleven o'clock. It was time. Leonidas grabbed the folder with a rude jerk, left his office, and strode resoundingly through the

long corridors of the old palace and up the magnificent
flight of stairs into the realm of the minister.

The Red Salon was a rather cramped, musty-smelling space
almost completely filled by its green conference table. Here
the more intimate meetings of the ministry were often held.
Four men were already present. With his stereotypical smile
(at once delighted and mocking) Leonidas greeted them.
First and foremost was the presiding "Chairman," the ministry's cabinet chief, Jaroslav Skutecky, a man in his mid-
sixties, the only one with seniority over Leonidas. Skutecky,
with his old-fashioned frock coat, his pointed, iron-gray
beard, his red hands, his harsh diction, was the polar opposite of the section chief, this man of fashion. He was
explaining, not without a certain air of enthusiasm, to two
younger undersecretaries and the red-haired Professor
Schummerer, how brilliantly he had arranged his yearly
summer vacation – with the whole, "woefully seven-headed"
family as he stressed time and again:

"At the most beautiful lake in the country, just imagine,
at the foot of our most majestic mountains, just imagine a
jewel box of a place, not too elegant but where you can get
your sap flowing, with outdoor swimming and dancing for
the younger set, with motor coaches going every which way
as you can imagine, and for angina and gout these well-
tended promenades. Three big rooms in the hotel, no luxury,
but water flowing hot and cold, and all the other essentials.
You gentlemen will not guess the price. No more than five
schillings per head. The dining, picture this, sumptuous,
splendid, a three-course lunch, a four-course supper. Listen:

Soup, appetizer, roast beef with two vegetables, a dessert, cheese, fruit, everything cooked in butter or the best drippings, on my word, I'm not making this up . . ."

Now and then this paean would be interrupted by affirmative grunts of admiration from the listeners, with a younger face, like a sponge with a snub nose, laudably outdoing the others. Leonindas, however, stepped to the window and stared at the soberly spiritual walls of the gothic Minorite Church across the way from the ministry palace. Thanks to Amelie, thanks to her childlessness, it had not been necessary for him to sink to the endless banality of middle-class life like old Skutecky and all his other colleagues who served out their preferential positions with exceedingly meager salaries. ("The civil servant possesses nothing, but that he has for life," so says one Viennese satirist.) Leonidas met the cool glass of the window with his forehead. On the left side of the crouching church, huddled a neglected little entry garden from whose grass a pair of rather scrawny acacia trees grew. The motionless leaves seemed deceptively copied from nature in wax. Today the beautiful enclosure resembled the gloomy airshaft of a tenement building. You could not see the sky. It became ever darker in the room. Leonidas had sunk so low in his distracted state that he had not noticed the arrival of the minister. Only the chipper, vaguely hoarse voice of Vincent Spittelberger woke him:

"Greetings to one and all, hello, gentlemen, hello . . ."

The minister was a little man in a crinkly, rumpled suit, which made one think its wearer had been sleeping in it for several nights. Everything on this Spittelberger was gray and curiously washed out. His crew-cut hair stood up. His cheeks had been badly shaven. His thick lips protruded.

His eyes had an eccentric squint – "heaven bent" one would say in this country. His pot belly stuck out with little warning and without foundation from under his modest ribcage. The man came from one of the Alpine districts and called himself a peasant in every other sentence, which was not the case for his entire life had been spent in big cities, twenty of them in the capital as a teacher and finally director of a night school. And Spittelberger gave the impression of a day-blind, nocturnal animal. The stubbornly old-fashioned pince-nez in front of his heaven-bent eyes seemed not to help him see. Immediately after taking the presiding chair at the conference table, his big head, full of attentive detachment, settled on his right shoulder. The others in the room knew that the minister had held a series of political rallies in the past few days throughout the country and had just arrived from a distant province on the night train in the wee hours. Spittelberger's nature was reputed to be always one of sleep deprived resilience:

"I have asked you gentlemen here," he began with a hoarse urgency, "because I would really like to have the matter of these appointments sewn up for tomorrow's ministerial council. You gentlemen know me. I'm expeditious. Thus, my dear Skutecky, if you please . . ."

With a half, almost throwaway gesture, he invited the officials to take their seats, while indicating to Professor Schummerer the place to his immediate right. This carrot-top played the role of ministry spy at the university and was considered the favorite of Spittelberger, the "Political Sphinx" as some called him. Much to Leonidas's annoyance, Schummerer always dropped in before noon, drifting around the building into various offices with his shuffling gait, holding up work while trading his academic gossip for the political kind. He was a prehistoric expert. His knowledge of history began exactly where history left off. In a way, his research interest was fishing in troubled waters. Schummerer's curiosity was not confined to the past. It was just as much in the present Stone Age. He possessed the finest ear for that web of connections, contacts, sympathies, and intrigues. Like a barometer, one could read his face for fluctuations in the political climate. To whichever side he leaned, there the power was tomorrow without fail . . .

"If Herr Section Chief would be so good . . ." said old Skutecky with his guttural pronunciation, looking inquiringly at the folder that lay before Leonidas.

"Of course," the so-named cleared his throat, opened the folder, and began with his twenty-five years of acquired technical proficiency in presentation. Six chairs had to be filled at different universities across the country. In the order, and according to the information on the records lying before him, the section chief reported on each of the scholars who had received recommendation. He did this with his consciousness split in two. Beside him his voice did a wonderful job as soloist. A deep silence prevailed. No one raised any objection to the candidates. Every time a case was settled, Leonidas handed the paper in question to the young, sponge-faced civil servant who stood officiously behind the minister and in whose enormous briefcase he carefully put the paper away. Vincent Spittelberger had even put his pince-nez down on the table and gone to sleep. He picked up sleep wherever and however he could, in fact, he hoarded it. A half-hour here, ten minutes there, together it amounted to a handsome sum from which one could draw without running up much of a deficit at night. The night was necessary for friends, for servicing this or that table reserved for regulars, for taking care of debts, for traveling, and for that incredible love of conspiracy. What had been planted during the day germinated in those chummy nights, the tender sprouts of intrigue. In other words, a politician in an exalted position could not dispense with the night, which, albeit a gypsy, is a productive element. One played a minister with a portfolio today. Tomorrow, perhaps, one seized total power in the country if he read the signs of the times correctly, recognized and not imprudently committed himself to this or that faction. Spittelberger slept a peculiar sleep that was like a curtain full of holes and tears that was no less refreshing. Behind it the sleeper lurked, ready to come out and grab someone at any moment.

Leonidas had spoken for twenty minutes, during which he read from the vitæ of the professors under consideration their achievements and works and gave an account of their political and civic good behavior from the latest reports. His pleasant voice breezed along softly, quickly. No one noticed, as it were, that his voice was assuming the risk and cost on its own, independent of the speaker's mind. The paperwork for the fifth sage had just now made its way into the hand of the sponge-face.

It had become so dark that somebody had switched on the ceiling lights. "I now come to our medical faculty," said the pleasant voice, making a pregnant pause.

"The professor of internal medicine, Herr Minister," Skutecky interjected in a bit raised but almost pious tone as if he were in church. This manner of waking Spittelberger was not necessary for he had opened his colorless eyes heavenward long ago and without a trace of incomprehension or drowsiness in the circles around them. This sleep artist could without a doubt recount the names and attributes of the previous five candidates under discussion better even than Leonidas.

"Medicine," he laughed, "keep your eyes on that. It's what interests the public. It's where you go from science into fortune-telling. I'm but a simple man, a harmless country fellow, as you gentlemen well know, that's why I like going straight to the herbalist, the faith healer, or the barber when something's a matter with me. But nothing's a matter with me . . ."

Schummerer, the paleontologist, snickered with facile exaggeration. He knew how conceited Spittelberger was about his jokes. Skutecky as well, backed by the subordinate grins of the younger men, gushed: "Can't top that . . ." Then he quickly added:

"So, Herr Minister will fall back on the nomination of Professor Lichtl . . ."

Having hit one bull's eye with his acknowledged wit, Spittelberger grinned and noticeably sucked in some saliva. "Have you no bigger church candles in stock," he said playing on the man's name, "than this teeny-weeny candle? If I've got any use for him, I'd make the devil himself Professor of Internal Medicine . . ."

Without taking part during all this time, Leonidas stared at a few pieces of paper that still lay before him. He read the name of the famous cardiologist Professor Alexander Bloch. His own hand had written the word "Impossible" over this name. The air was thick with a pall of cigarette smoke and filtered light. One could hardly breathe.

"The faculty and the academic senate have unanimously

given their support to Lichtl," Schummerer said, affirming Skutecky's suggestion, and nodded, certain of winning his way. But then rose the voice of section chief Leonidas, "Impossible."

Everyone suddenly looked up. Spittelberger's naturally sleepy face brightened with curiosity.

"I beg your pardon," asked the old chairman coarsely, believing he had misunderstood his colleague. Only yesterday Skutecky had spoken to the section chief about this delicate case and how, in these times, it would be impossible to entrust an important chair to Professor Alexander Bloch no matter how well qualified. Leonidas had been entirely of the same opinion and had made no secret as well of his dislike for Professor Bloch given his well-known cheerleaders. And now? The gentlemen present were surprised, even dismayed by this remarkably dramatic "Impossible." Not least of all was Leonidas.

While his voice had calmly left the interjection to be explained, the other person inside him found it almost amusing: I am becoming entirely unfaithful to myself and have already begun delivering for my son . . . "I don't want Dr. Lichtl," he said loudly. "He may be a good doctor and teacher, but he only served in the provinces, his publications are insubstantial, one knows nothing about him. Professor Bloch, however, is a world-renowned Nobel Prize-winner in medicine, a doctor honored by eight European and American universities. He is a physician to kings and heads of state. Just a few weeks ago someone had called him to London for a consultation at Buckingham Palace. Year in and year out he sees the wealthiest patients in Vienna, Argentinean nabobs, and Indian maharajahs. A small country like ours cannot afford to ignore and insult such a great man. We risk turning public opinion against us throughout the western hemisphere by this insult . . ."

A shadow of contempt flitted across the mouth of the speaker. He knew he had been asked recently about the "Bloch case" at a glittering social event. During the course of that evening the same arguments that he used now had been rejected by him most peremptorily. Such international success as Bloch's and his gang was not based on real value and achievements, but rather on the reciprocal promotion among the Israelites of the world, on that of its slavish press, on that notorious snowball system of unflinching self-advertisement. These were not only his words, but his convictions as well.

Schummerer the paleontologist awkwardly wiped his brow.

"That's all well and good, my dear Herr Section Chief . . . Unfortunately the private life of this gentleman is not perfect. You know, an inveterate gambler, night after night, poker and baccarat. This concerns enormous sums. We have a police report about it. And this gentleman knows how to collect his fees, I'll drink to that, he's notorious. Anywhere from two hundred to a thousand schillings, and that's only for the initial examination. He only has a heart for his coreligionists, as everyone knows, whom he treats for free, especially if they enter the office wearing a caftan . . . For my part, I think that a little country like ours cannot afford even one Abraham Bloch . . ."

At this point old Skutecky took over for the far too agitated prehistorian. He did so with a completely objective, nonjudgmental tone of voice:

"I ask you to consider that Professor Alexander Bloch is

already sixty-seven years old and has only two more years of active teaching left if one does not consider his honorary year-off before retirement."

Leonidas, unstoppable on this slope, could not leave unsaid any jest then in vogue among certain circles in the city:

"Yes, indeed, gentleman. Before he was too young for tenure. Now he is too old. And somewhere in between he had the misfortune to be *stuck* with the name *Abraham* Bloch . . ."

Nobody laughed. The furrowed brows of these crossword-solvers regarded their renegade. What was going on here? What dark forces were mixed up in this performance? Of course, the husband of a Paradini – one blessed by so much money and influence would have the nerve to swim against the tide. The Paradinis belonged to international society. Aha! So the wind blows. This Abraham Bloch really does set heaven and hell in motion and probably the English royals as well. Machinations of freemasonry and the international gold cartel while the likes of us have no idea where we'll get the money for a new suit . . .

The redheaded talebearer blew his porous nose and thoughtfully contemplated the findings:

"Our big neighbor," he said sounding resigned and threatening at the same time, "has cleaned out its colleges and universities of radical and foreign elements. If Bloch gets a professorship from us, and for internal medicine, it is a demonstration, it's punching the Reich's nose. I would like to impress that on Herr Minister . . . And in defense of our freedom, we do want to take the wind from those people's sails, don't we . . ."

This allegory of the wind, to take it from the sails of the future helmsman, was quite popular in those days. Someone said: "Quite right!" It was the sponge-faced subaltern getting carried away, chiming in from behind the Minister's chair. Leonidas fixed a penetrating stare on him. The fellow belonged to a department that the section chief rarely came in contact with. The inscrutable Spittelberger, however, had made him one of his favorites, which was why he had drawn his present assignment as a consultant. Leonidas could hardly stand the transparent expression of the fat boy, the way it radiated such hate. Just the name "Abraham Bloch" was inflammatory enough to turn that broad, phlegmatic face an angry red. From what sources had this abundance of hate gathered itself? And why had it, with such cheek, with such openness, turned on him, the most proven man in the place, who could look back on twenty-five honorable years of service? Personally, he had never shown the least preference for types such as Professor Bloch. On the contrary! He avoided, if not strongly refused, to have anything to do with them. But now he saw himself immediately – as strange as it might seem – wrapped up with this fishy community. All of it due to Vera Wormser's diabolical letter. The secure foundations of his existence were being turned on end. He found himself being forced to represent the candidacy of some fashionable medical idol against his convictions. And now Leonidas had to put up with every unapologetic remark and the shameless looks of that cheeky, spongy creature as though he were not only Bloch's defender but Bloch himself. It was happening so fast.

Leonidas was first to lower his eyes before this enemy who suddenly rose against him. Only then did he feel Spittelberger staring at him attentively over the top of his crooked pince-nez:

"Remarkable, you have changed your point of view, Herr Section Chief . . ."

"Yes, Herr Minister, I did change my opinion on the matter . . ."

"In politics, dear friend, sometimes it is good to stir up trouble. It just depends on whom you stir up . . ."

"I don't have the honor to be a politician, Herr Minister. In the service of the state I can only do my best . . ."

A frosty pause. Skutecky and the other civil servants squirmed inside themselves. But Spittelberger did not seem to be put out by the barbed statement. He displayed his bad teeth and explained good-naturedly:

"Don't worry, I meant that only as a simple man, as an old peasant . . ."

There was no person in the whole wide world – as Leonidas felt now – who was less simple, who was more sneaky, more convoluted than this "old peasant." Behind the soundproof brow of his thick bristled skull, on many floors built one upon the other, the elevated and the underground railroads of his tireless determination raced perceptibly. Spittelberger's electric opportunism was like a cloudscape in the room, more tormenting than even Schummerer's and the sponge-face's hostility. The last breathable air was gone.

"Herr Minister, permit me," Leonidas snapped and opened a window. In that same instant the downpour burst. A wall of water sheeted down in fine hash marks. You could no longer see the Minorite Church. The din of a cavalry charge clattered over the roofs and cobblestones. In the midst of this giant hall of rain, thunder rumbled without lightning leading the way.

"That was high time," said Skutecky with his harsh pro-nunciation.

Spittelberger stood up. With his left shoulder hunched up, with both hands in the pockets of his crinkled trousers, he made his sluggish way toward Leonidas. Now he really did look like a peasant, at the weekend market, trying to get rid of his overpriced cow:

"How about it, Herr Section Chief, if we let this Bloch have the gold Cross of Honor for Art and Science and the title of Privy Counsel as well . . ."

This suggestion evinced how the Minister did not regard his section chief as an office boy like the good Jaroslav Skutecky, but rather as an influential personality behind whom obscure powers concealed themselves and could not be touched. The solution to this problem was worthy of Spittelberger. A department chair and a teaching hospital, they stood for positions of real power and should not be taken away from the homegrown talent. A big medal, however, one seldom awarded, represented an honor of such rank that the opposition party would no longer be able to open their traps. Both sides get something.

"What do you think of this way out?" tempted Spittelberger.

"I consider that way out impermissible, Herr Minister," Leonidas replied.

Vincent Spittelberger, the Sphinx, planted his thickset legs far apart and lowered his gray, bristle brush head like a goat. Leonidas observed a bald spot on his crown and heard the politician sucking on his saliva before calmly pointing out:

"My dear friend, you know I am very expeditious . . ."

"I cannot stop Herr Minister from making a mistake," Leonidas said curtly while this intoxicating awareness of some unknown courage flowed through him. What's going on? For Alexander (Abraham) Bloch? Absurd! This unfortunate Bloch was only a cause that could be exchanged for another. But Leonidas fancied himself strong enough for the truth now, for the renewal of his life.

Minister Spittelbeger had already left the Red Salon followed by Skutecky and the other ministerial staff. Without let up, the rain beat down.

FIFTH CHAPTER

A Confession, But Not the Right One

When Leonidas came home, it was still raining steadily, though now it fell in tired streaks. The butler informed him that Madam had not yet returned from her drive. It seldom ever happened that Leonidas, coming from the office in the afternoon, had to wait for Amelie. As he slipped his wet coat onto a hanger, the uneasiness over his current behavior still tingled. By opposing the Minister he had lost that discretion of official procedure for the first time in his life. A good civil servant did not fight with an open visor. You skillfully, prudently used the course of world events to carry you along so as to avoid undesirable rocks and make for those desirable spots to put ashore. But he had been unfaithful to this refined art and had botched the case of Alexander (Abraham) Bloch, stirring up a crisis over it, a cabinet crisis. (And to Leonidas the whole thing was a yawning bore.) Instead of drifting along, secretly influenced by Vera and this son in the struggle, he should have been in control of the "negative method" in the time-honored tradition. Rather than be *for* Professor Bloch, he needed to be *against* Professor Lichtl, not for any real reason, but purely on formal grounds. Skutecky had once again proven himself the master at the meeting, not leading the charge against Bloch with sheer anti-Semitism, but rather on the objective and fair reasons of his advanced age. In a similar way, he should have constructed the argument that the nomination of Lichtl did not meet all the competencies. Should the Council of Ministers decide to go with the appointment of this spacefiller, then he, the section chief, had incurred a profound defeat on his turf. It was too late now. His actions today, his defeat tomorrow – soon they would inevitably force him into retirement. In a flash he saw the sponge-face filled with hate. It was the look, the hate of a generation that had made a fanatical decision and was intent on exterminating "unreliables," such as the section chief, without mercy. Insult the vengeful Spittelberger, make the blood boil for the sponge-face and the other younger people ... just think about it, it's enough to end everything. Leonidas, who had taken such an astonished joy in his career that morning, gave it up now without a struggle at half past noon, and with no regrets. The rest of the day called for a transformation that was all too much. And the hour of his approaching confession weighed all too heavily. He had to go through with it.

Slowly he climbed the staircase to the upper floor. As always, his terry bathrobe hung over the back of the chair, laid out ready. He took off his gray jacket and washed his hands and face in the bathroom. Then, with comb and brush, he redid his perfect part. As he regarded his youthfully thick hair in the mirror, the strangest feeling came over him. These well-groomed good looks, those of a younger man, made him feel sorry for himself. Nature's incomprehensible unfairness, which condemned the sleeper on the Schönbrunn Park bench to fall apart at fifty, had blessed him with this freshness of youth that now seemed senselessly wasted on him. By having all of his soft, thick hair, his pink cheeks, he had been thrown off course. It would have been easier for him had he seen an old, wasted face starring out from the mirror. But his familiar face, his cherished features, presented him with all there was to lose as the sun still rose so opulently high . . .

With his hands behind his back, he sauntered through the upstairs rooms. In Amelie's dressing room he stood sniffing the air. He very seldom entered this part of the house. The perfume, the one that Amelie liked the most, gently assaulted him like an accusation whose effect is redoubled by its subtlety. The fragrance added anew to the burden of his heart. An undertone of burned hair and rubbing alcohol intensified his melancholy. A sprinkle of disorder, which Amelie had left in her wake, still prevailed. Several pairs of petite shoes lay about in a sad disarrangement. The dressing table, with its many little containers, crystal perfume bottles, jewelry boxes, makeup jars, nail clippers, files, brushes, seemed hardly deserted. Like the tender impression of a body left behind on pillows, so Amelie's existence pervaded the room. On her desk, next to books, photo weeklies, and fashion magazines, piles of open letters were left carelessly on display. It was stupid, but in this minute Leonidas wished Amelie had done something to him, that he could feel some unspeakable pain, that she would have the guilty conscience weighing on her. It would almost restore the innocence to his. Something he had always abhorred he did now for the first time. He fell upon the open letters and excitedly rooted through the cold paper, reading a line here, a sentence there, seizing upon any masculine handwriting, searching for evidence of adultery, a most unlikely treasure hunter of what he was guilty of. Was it possible that for all these twenty years Amelie had remained a faithful wife to him, a pathetic coward, the most tireless of liars who had forever hid the misery of his miserable youth beneath the cracking, rambling varnish of a lot of phony talk? He had never been able to close the divinely ordained distance between him and her, the distance between a born Paradini and a born bottom-feeder. He alone knew that his security, his dandyish manner, his casual elegance were derived from others, a laborious disguise from which not even sleep released him. With beating heart he looked for letters from the man who would make him the cuckold. What he found were the purest orgies of innocence that made nothing but good-natured fun of him. He tore open the drawers of the graceful little desk. A lovely, feminine chaos of things forgotten presented itself. Among scraps of velvet and silk, genuine and costume jewelry, Bakelite bracelets, mateless gloves, calling cards, silk flowers, lipstick, pillboxes, and petrified chocolates lay bundles of old invoices tied with string, bank statements, and once more letters – these too innocently smiled and laughed at him. At last a datebook fell into his hand. He leafed through it. Without shame he violated this secret – Amelie's fleeting entries on certain days: "Alone again today with Leon! Finally! Thank God!" "After the theater a wonderful night. Like once in May. Leon charming." In this little diary a moving, exacting balance book of their love had been recorded. The final entry took up several lines: "Find something changed in Leon since his birthday. He is somewhat hurtfully gallant, condescending, inattentive. This is a dangerous age for men. I must keep an eye on him. No! I have total faith." The word *total* was underlined three times.

She believed in him. How trusting she was despite her

jealousy. His absurd fear, his soiled hope had been self-deception. No guilt on her part would release him from his. In fact, with her faith, she had really saddled his soul with the greatest burden of them all. Served him right. Leonidas sat down at the desk and stared thoughtlessly at the sweet disorder that he had defiled and spread about with his rude hand.

He did not jump in fear, he remained sitting when Amelie appeared.

"What are you doing here?" she asked. The shadows and bluish cast under her eyes had become more noticeable. Leonidas showed no sign of embarrassment. What a cunning liar I am, he thought, there really is no situation that trips me up. He turned a tired face to her:

"I was looking for something to take for my headache. Aspirin or Pyramidon . . ."

"There's a box of Pyramidon in front of you big as day . . ."

"My god, I must have overlooked it . . ."

"Perhaps you have been too busy with my correspondence . . . after all, my dear, a woman as messy as me surely has nothing to hide . . ."

"No, Amelie, I know how you are, I have total faith in you . . ." He stood up, wanting to take her hand. She drew back a step and said rather pointedly:

"It isn't exactly gallant when a husband is far too trusting of his wife . . ."

Leonidas pressed his fists against his temples. The headache he'd just been faking had promptly made its appearance. She had something, she was on to him. Since this morning she had something. And since then it seemed to have congealed. If she makes one of her scenes, if she gets abusive and browbeats me, then my confession will be easier to make. But if she goes soft and tender on me, then I know I won't have the courage . . . Hell – there can be no more ifs, ands, or buts, I have to talk.

Amelie pulled her violet-purple gloves off by the fingers, put down her summery, sheer full-length coat, then she silently took a tablet from the pillbox, went into the bathroom, and returned with a glass of water. Oh no, she is going to be good to me. Damn. As she dissolved the drug in a spoon, she asked:

"Did something upset you today?"

"Yes, I had a problem. At work."

"Spittelberger, of course? I can well imagine."

"Amelie, let's not talk about that . . ."

"This Vincent looks like a dried-up toad before it rains. And Herr Skutecky, that Czech village schoolmaster! The kind of people allowed to lord over us these days . . ."

"The princes and counts of former times looked better, but governed far worse. You're an incurable aesthete, Amelie . . ."

"You don't really have to put up with this, León. You don't need these ordinary people. Toss it back at them . . ."

She placed the spoon to his lips, handed him the glass. His heart suddenly dropped with longing. He wanted to pull her to himself. She tilted her head to one side. He noted that she must have spent at least two hours at the salon. Her hair was impeccably permed into a cloud and smelled like love itself. This is madness, what have I to do with that ghost Vera Wormser. Amelie looked at him sternly:

"I insist from now on, Leon, that you rest daily for one hour after every meal. When all is said and done, you're at that dangerous age for men . . ."

Leonidas seized on her words as though they might serve for his defense:

"Right you are, darling ... Today I learned that fifty years old is really old."

"Silly," she laughed without being sharp. "It would be fine with me if you were an older man once and for all and not this notorious, eternal pretty boy every woman gapes at ..."

The bell rang for dinner. Downstairs, in the large dining room, there was a little round side table placed by the window. The great family table in the middle of the room stood with its twelve high-backed chairs empty and lifeless – no, worse – dead without having lived. Leonidas and Amelie had no family. They sat as though banished from their own family table, at the tea table of childlessness. And Amelie too seemed to feel this exile today more than yesterday, along with all the other yesterdays and years, because she said:

"If it's okay with you, after today I'll have the table set upstairs in the living room ..."

Leonidas nodded absentmindedly. All of his senses were tightening for the first words of the confession he was about to make. Then a crazy idea lit up inside him. What if he, in the course of his big confession, instead of begging for forgiveness, cut the leash and smoothly demanded from Amelie that she accept his son in their home, that he live with them, and that he eat at the same table. Surely a child by him and Vera must have some qualities. And wouldn't a young, happy face bring a glow to their lives?

The first course was being served. Leonidas piled his plate full, but put down his fork after the third bite. The butler had not handed the serving dish to Amelie, but had instead set a bowl of raw celery stalks next to her place setting. Instead of the second course, she only received a tiny, seared cutlet without condiments or anything to give it flavor. Leonidas looked at her surprised:

"Are you not feeling well, Amelie, where's your appetite?"

Her look could not hide bitter resentment:

"I'm dying of hunger," she said.

"That sparrow's portion isn't going to satisfy you."

She poked around in her salad, which had been specially prepared for her without oil and vinegar, just a few drops of lemon juice:

"Is today the first time you've noticed," she asked pointedly, "that I live like a saint in the desert?"

He replied rather voicelessly and awkwardly:

"And what kind of kingdom of heaven will this get you?"

She pushed the salad away from her in disgust:

"A ridiculous heaven, my dear. For it really doesn't matter what I look like to you ... It makes no difference to you if I look like a ballerina or a barrel ..."

In keeping with his bad day, Leonidas dug an ever deeper hole of saying the wrong thing:

"To me you're just fine, darling, just the way you are ... You overrate my sense of decorum ... And you don't have to live like a saint for my sake ..."

Her eyes, which were older than herself, flashed at him, filling with an ugly, seething rage:

"Aha, so I'm already beyond good and evil. You're thinking that nothing can help me, that I'm nothing more than an old bad habit for you, one you can't shake. A bad habit that has its practical side ..."

"For heaven's sake, Amelie, think about what you're saying ..."

Amelie had no intention of thinking about what she was saying. She just poured it out:

67

"And just a moment ago, silly goose me, I was almost happy that you were disgustingly spying in my letters . . . He's jealous after all, I thought . . . But no . . . You were probably curious about more valuable things than just love letters because you looked so evasive that it scared me so, . . . you were like a conman, like a gentleman-swindler, like a seducer of servant girls on Sunday . . ."

"Thanks," Leonidas said and looked at his plate. Amelie could not control herself any longer and broke into a loud sob. There would now be a scene. An appalling and totally pointless scene. Never before has she expressed herself like this against me with such dead-on suspicion. Against me – he who insisted on a strict division, he who left the room when she received her bankers and lawyers. And yet she shoots wide and hits a bull's-eye nevertheless. A seducer of servant girls on Sunday. Her anger doesn't make it any easier for me. I have no chance of beginning . . . Besieged he rose, stepped toward Amelie, and took her hand:

"I really don't want to understand this silly talk that you're having with me . . . Your damned fixation on counting calories is going to make you a nervous wreck . . . Please pull yourself together . . . We don't want to put on a comedy in front of people . . ."

This reminder brought her to herself. The butler could enter at any moment:

"Forgive me, Leon, I beg you," she stammered while sobbing, "I've been so very miserable today, this weather, the hairdresser, and then . . ."

She was once more in control, pressing her napkin to her eyes, gritting her teeth. The butler, an older man, brought the coffee, cleared away the fruit plate, the fingerbowls, and seemed to take no notice. For a rather long time he busied himself with an earnest apathy as the couple said nothing. When they were alone again, Leonidas asked offhandedly: "Do you have some particular reason for mistrusting me?"

While he breathlessly asked this question with a furtive soul, he felt as though he were throwing a gangplank over a dark crevasse. Amelie gave him a desperate look with her red eyes:

"Yes, I have a particular reason, León . . ."

"And may I know this reason?"

"I know you can't stand me when I interrogate you. Leave me alone. Maybe I can get over it . . ."

"But if I don't get over it," he said gently, yet stressing each word. She struggled with herself for a little while, then lowered her head:

"You got a letter this morning . . ."

"I received eleven letters this morning . . ."

"But one of them was from a woman . . . Such a deceptive, deceitful woman's handwriting . . ."

"You really found the handwriting deceitful?" Leonidas asked taking his hands out of his pockets very slowly and producing for her the corpus delicti. Moving his chair a little away from the table toward the window, he let the rain-spotted light fall on Vera's letter. The balance of fate stood still in the room. How everything takes its own course. You don't need to worry. You don't even have to improvise. Everything comes out differently, but it comes of its own accord. Our future will depend on whether she can read between the lines. Suddenly becoming the casual observer, he handed the narrow sheet of paper to Amelie with an outstretched hand.

She took it. She read. She read half-aloud: "To the esteemed Herr Section Chief." Already, with these words of address, her features relaxed with such an expressive power of a kind Leonidas had never seen before in Amelie. He heard her take a deep breath. Then she read on even louder:

"I have forced myself now to turn to you for a favor. It does not concern me, but rather a young talented man . . ."

A talented young man. Amelie put the letter down on the table without reading further. She started crying again. She laughed. Laughter and sobs mixed together. Then the laughter spread through her and filled her like an element with a tongue of fire. Suddenly she jumped up, fell before Leonidas, and, crouching at his feet, put her head on his knees, an act of her submission, her devotional hours. However, because she was so tall and had such long legs, this impassioned act of humiliation always took him aback a little. It made him shudder now.

"If you were a cave man," she stammered, "you would have to beat me or strangle me now or whatever, for I hated you so much, my darling, like I've never hated before. Don't say anything, for God's sake, let me confess . . ."

He said nothing. He let her confess. He regarded her blond, softly coiffed hair. She spoke rapidly without looking up once, as though deep into the earth:

"When you're sitting at the hairdresser's with your head under that nickel-plated hood for hours, it hums in your ears, the air keeps getting hotter, every single root screams with the tension, you put up with it because you want this nice wave, because of the opera this evening, because this weather's always messing up your hair . . . I flip through the pictures in *Vogue* and *Jardin des Modes* without seeing anything, just to keep from going crazy because, you see, I was totally convinced that you were a lifelong swindler, a slick con artist, some kind of Sunday housemaid seducer, always

70

tip-top, a slippery eel, and you had me deceived for twenty full years, 'under false pretenses,' isn't that what they say in court, for you had been playing me since the day of our engagement and I've wasted my entire life and youth to catch on to you, that you have a mistress named 'Vera Wormser c/o' because I found her letter on the table just moments before you came to breakfast and it was like this horrible revelation, and it took all of my strength to keep myself from stealing that letter, but that was unnecessary because I already could see right through it that you were leading a double life like you see in the movies, and you have a house, an idyllic life together, you and 'Vera Wormser c/o,' for how would I know what you do at the office all the time and at meetings deep into the night, and you have children together, two or maybe even three . . . And I have seen the house, on my word, somewhere in Döbling, in the neighborhood of Kugler Park or Wertheimstein Park because children always need fresh air, I was right there inside this charming home that you furnished for this woman, and I recovered a few knickknacks that I had been missing, and I also saw your children, right there were three, such nasty, half-grown bastards, and they jumped all around you calling you 'Uncle' sometimes and sometimes calling you 'Papa' without any shame, you listen in on their schoolwork and the littlest one climbed all over you for you're a happy daddy, the storybook kind. All this is happening to me while my head is trapped under the hairdryer and I can't run away, instead I have to be gracious when the sudsy salon owner just had to amuse me – *Frau Section Chief, you look dazzling, will Frau Section Chief have a part in the Schönbrunn Costume Festival, Frau Section Chief must be appearing as the young Empress Maria Theresa in a hoop skirt and a towering white wig, no lady of the aristocracy can vie with Frau Section Chief, Herr Section Chief will be impressed* – and I could not tell him that I really don't want to impress Herr Section Chief because he's a crook and a happy daddy in Döbling . . . Don't say a word, let me come clean for the worst is yet to come. I not only hated you, Leon, I was scared to death of you. Your double life stood before me like, like, I don't know what it was like, but at the same time, Leon, I was so horribly certain, in a way I can't describe anymore, that you wanted to kill me, because you had to get rid of me no matter what because you couldn't kill Vera Wormser, she's the mother of your children, this anyone can see, but I'm only connected to you by a marriage certificate, a piece of paper, consequently you will kill me and you'll do it with such skill, with a slow-working poison, in daily doses, best dripped into my salad the way people in the Renaissance did, the Borgias, and so on. You don't feel a thing, just get more anemic and paler by the day until it's over. Oh, I swear to you, Leon, I saw myself lying in my coffin, wonderfully laid out by you, and I was so young and charming with my hair freshly permed, dressed entirely in white, in a flowing, pleated silk crepe gown, but don't think I'm saying this ironically or being funny – my heart was broken when I saw too late that the man I loved passionately, whom I passionately trusted, is a wife killer. And then they all came, of course, the minister, the president, the top government people, everyone who's anyone, to pay their respects and your performance was monstrously impeccable for you were wearing your tuxedo, just like when we first met, you remember, at the Solicitors Ball, then you walked over to the president, just behind my coffin, no, you strode, and winked at Vera Wormser watching with her children from a grandstand . . . So just imagine, Leon, I came home with these pictures in my head and then find you with my letters, something that has never happened in all these twenty years. I could not believe my eyes and this was no longer a figment of my imagination for you were not you, but a total stranger, the man with the double life, this husband to another, this gentleman-swindler when no-one's watching. I don't know if you can forgive me, but at that very moment it was like being struck by lightning: He wants nothing but to secure that enormous fortune after my death. Yes, Leon, this is what you looked like, upstairs, at my desk, with the open drawer, like someone surprised forging a will, a legacy hunter. And I still haven't even thought about making a will. And yes everything belongs to you. Shut up! Let me get it all out, all of it, everything! Afterwards you must punish me as my stern priest, my confessor. Give me a terrible penance. You could, one of these days, see Anita Hoyos by yourself. She's crazy about you and your eyes eat her up. I will patiently remain at home and not henpeck you for I know perfectly well you're not to blame for those horrid fantasies of this morning. It's my fault, and that letter from this innocent lady Wormser – whose handwriting looks hostile by the way. The craftiest husband could never, ever – there's no other word for it – dream like this, the way a wife does under a hairdryer at the salon. Well, I'm not the hysterical kind, I'm even rather smart, and you thought so too once. You must understand me, I knew all the while you couldn't lead a double life and the money doesn't interest you and you are this most distinguished person, a celebrated educator of young people, and the entire world honors you and you are way above me. But at the same time I knew very well you're devious, a cheat, and my sweet, beloved poisoner. It was, believe me, not jealousy, it came from outside

73

of me, it was like an inspiration. And then I got you a glass
of water and with my own hand prepared the Pyramidon for
my poisoner to swallow and my heart bled with love and
disgust, it's true, Leon, as I have proved myself . . . So now I
have confessed everything to you. What happened to me
today I don't understand. Perhaps you can explain it to me?"

Without looking up, without paragraph and period,
always at the ground, Amelie rushed through her confession, only interrupting her harping with an ironic twist out
of burning shame. Never before had Leonidas heard such
self-revelation or known that this woman was capable of it.
Now she pressed her face against his knees, letting her tears
flow without holding back. He began to feel this warm, wet
sensation through the thin material of his trousers. It was
unpleasant and at the same time quite touching. You're right,
my child. It was real insight that came to you today, that did
not let go the whole morning long. Vera's letter had inspired
you. How close you fluttered around the flame of truth.
I can't explain your clairvoyance. That is, I'd finally have to
say something now. I'd have to start out: You're right, my
little girl. How very strange it is, you've got real insight . . .
But can I talk like this now? Could a man, one with far more
character than I, ever talk like this now?

"That really wasn't very attractive of you," he said aloud,
"to let your old jealousy dream up something against me.
But as a teacher I do have some official expertise about the
human soul. I long sensed your being on edge. We'll soon
have lived together for twenty years and have only suffered
one long separation, you and I. These inevitable crises do
come up, one today, another tomorrow. It was incredibly
moral of you to come straight with me about your slander-

ously subconscious mind. I envy you for your confession. Now, I almost forgot, do you really think that I'm a poisoner, that I'd forge a will ..."

And so my sanctimonious lies go on. I haven't forgotten a thing. The seducer of servant girls on Sunday, how fitting. Amelie lifted her face with an expression of transfigured attentiveness:

"Isn't it funny how indescribably happy you are after you've confessed and been forgiven? Everything's gone now ..."

Leonidas peered intently to one side while his hand gently stroked her hair:

"Yes, it's probably an enormous relief to have confessed from so deep inside. And you've not sinned in the least ..."

Amelie was taken aback. Suddenly she looked at him coolly, inquiringly:

"Why are you so terribly good, so wise, so remote, like it's nothing, like you're the purest Tibetan monk? Wouldn't it be nobler of you to take your revenge with a terrible confession of your own? ..."

It would certainly be nobler, he thought, and his silence became very deep. Only an irresolute cough left his mouth. Amelie was standing. She carefully powdered herself and applied lipstick. It was that feminine breathing space that closes a thrilling performance of real life. Once more her eyes regarded Vera's letter, that harmless letter of request, which lay on the table:

"It's not so bad, León," she hesitated, "but there is one thing that still bothers me ... Why did you carry this letter around in your wallet, of all today's mail, from this bizarre stranger?"

"This lady is no stranger to me," he replied seriously, curtly, "I knew her a long time ago. I worked in her father's house as a tutor during the lowest point in my life . . ."

He picked up the letter with a harsh, indeed, an ill-tempered jerk and put it back in his billfold.

"Then you should do something for her talented young man," said Amelie, and a warm dreamy look came to her April eyes.

SIXTH CHAPTER

Vera Appears and Vanishes

Immediately after lunch Leonidas left his house and drove to the Ministry. There he sat holding his head in his hands, staring far out the high window over the trees of the Volksgarten, which rose veiled in the rain's pearlescent mist into a patchwork sky. His heart was filled with wonder and admiration for Amelie. Women in love possessed a sixth sense. As it is with roaming deer against their enemies, so did they have the advantage of reliably sensing things. They were clairvoyants of masculine guilt. Amelie had guessed everything when she, in keeping with her kind, had exaggerated, distorted, and misinterpreted everything. You could almost think that an inexplicable conspiracy had existed between the two women, the one embodied in her pale blue handwriting, the other wounded in the heart by a fleeting glance at that same writing. In those few lines of his address Vera had whispered the truth to the other, which had to be felt by Amelie like a sudden intuition out of thin air. How incompatible this was given that clairvoyance, which failed her before the dry words of the letter. Nevertheless she had torn, both suspecting and unsuspecting, the mask from his face. "A seducer of servant girls on Sunday." And yet hadn't he called himself a marriage swindler today? And wasn't it really in the criminal sense of the word? Amelie could see it in his face. And yet a little while ago, when he had looked at himself in the mirror, he had discovered nothing so low as that. There was just his well-tempered dignity, which aroused this strange self-pity. And then how, without his help, had his resolve been turned around so that it was not him who confessed but rather her? That confession – an incredible, an undeserved testimony of love. He never had this radical, indeed, this brazen courage for truth as Amelie did, which probably came from his inferior background, his former poverty. His youth had been one occupied with anxiety, with striving, and a trembling overestimation of the upper class. He had had to frantically teach himself everything – the way to enter a room, a command of small talk (of making conversation), effortlessly fine table manners, the correct measure of "The-Honor-of-Requesting" and "The-Honor-of-Accepting" – all these fine and natural virtues that members of the gentleman caste are born with. The fifty-year-old still came from a world of forced class distinction. The stamina, which today's youth exerted in sports, he had had to expend on a special kind of athleticism – overcoming his shyness and reconciling his relentless feelings of deficiency. Oh, that unforgettable hour when he, as the victor, faced himself in the mirror for the first time in the jacket of the suicide victim. Even though he had learned to perfect those refined and self-confident arts, had practiced them unconsciously for decades, he was only what the Romans called a "freedman." And a freed slave doesn't have the natural courage for the truth, not like a born Paradini, not this bold transcendence over any shame. Moreover Amelie had recognized this freedman was at the edge of an abyss deeper than he knew himself. Yes, it was true, he was afraid of her anger, her revenge if he should acknowledge his and Vera's son. He feared she would immediately serve him with divorce papers. He feared nothing more than the loss of the wealth, which he enjoyed so nonchalantly. He, the man of class who "had nothing to do with money," the high official, the nation's educator, he knew now that he could not endure the narrow existence of his colleagues, this daily struggle to get the better things in life. He was all too spoiled by money and by the pleasant habit of not having to say no to the least impulse. He knew now why so many friends at work succumbed to temptation and accepted bribes so that they could provide their obsessed wives with some joy now and then. His head sank on his legal pad. He had this burning desire to be a monk, to belong to a strict order . . .

Leonidas needed to be a man about it. "You can't avoid it," he said loud and vacuously. Then he took a sheet of paper and started drafting a memo for Minister Vincent Spittelberger in which he attempted to justify entrusting *Associate* Professor of Medicine Alexander (Abraham) Bloch with the vacant chair and a teaching hospital as inevitably necessary for the state. He had no idea why he continued to press stubbornly and wanted a showdown, a test of strength. But he had barely committed ten lines to paper when he laid down his fountain pen and rang his secretary:

"Be a good fellow, will you, and call the Park Hotel in Hietzing and let Frau, or rather Fraulein Dr. Vera Wormser know that I will see her in person at four o'clock . . ."

As always in nervous moments, Leonidas had spoken with a flat, indistinct voice. His secretary placed an empty slip of paper before him:

"If you could please, Herr Section Chief, write down the

name of the lady for me," he said. For a long moment Leonidas stared at him without saying a word. Then he shoved the memo he had started into his briefcase and, taking leave, put everything on his desk into its right place and stood up:

"No thanks. It's not necessary. I'm leaving now."

The secretary felt obliged to remind that Herr Minister was expected back in the building around five o'clock. To Leonidas, who just took his hat and coat off the hook, this news seemed to have made no impression:

"If the Minister should ask for me, tell him nothing, tell him simply, I've gone away . . ."

With that he left his office, going by the younger man with a spring to his step.

Among the carefully considered conventions of the section chief was that he never nosed his big car into the Ministry by way of the main gate but rather, if he used it at all, alighted on Herrengasse. He feared more than just the envy of his colleagues, he considered it (especially during work hours) "tactless" to show off his material good fortune and conspicuously breach the Spartan boundaries of the civil service. Ministers, politicians, movie stars were allowed to calmly spread themselves out in shining limousines for they were creatures of self-advertisement. A section chief, however, was obliged (with all permissible elegance) to emphasize a certain austere economy. This stress on economy was perhaps one of the most intolerable forms of human vanity. How often he had with every requisite caution sought to convince Amelie that her cheerfully inexhaustible expenditures on jewelry and clothes did not completely correspond to his position. A futile lecture. She laughed at him. Herein lay one of life's conflicts that often left Leonidas bemused

... This time he took the streetcar, which let him off in the vicinity of the Schönbrunn Palace.

The rain had been letting up for an hour and had now stopped. But it was only that tedious pause in an illness, that dreary eye of painlessness between two bouts. The cloudy day hung at half mast, wet and limp, and every one of those strangely slowed-down minutes seemed to ask: *We've come this far, but where to now?* Leonidas felt in every nerve that vital change the world had undergone since that morning. He now realized the cause of this change as he hurried through the broad, plane tree-lined street along the high palace wall. Under his feet, swishing away most unpleasantly, was a thick carpet of wet fallen leaves. Newly turned, they resembled bloated bodies and burst with each step such that one might think a plague of frogs had rained down. In the last few hours more than half the leaves on the trees had blown away and the rest drooped from their branches. What had started as an early April morning had, with the wave of a hand, ended in a late November evening.

In the flower stand on the next street corner, Leonidas dithered impermissibly far too long between white and red roses. He finally decided on eighteen long-stemmed pale yellow tea roses whose gentler, delicately fermented scent appealed to him. In the hotel foyer, while giving his name at the desk for Frau Dr. Wormser, he was suddenly shocked by the betrayal in the number "eighteen," which he had unconsciously selected. Eighteen years. Then that ominous bunch of roses occurred to him, which he – the ridiculous, the love-struck – had once brought for Vera without finding the courage to give them to her. It was as now, for they had been pale yellow tea roses then, and they had been just as fragrant, as gentle, as full, like the bouquet of some paradisiacal wine not of this world.

"Madam asks that Herr Section Chief wait here," the porter said deferentially and escorted the guest into one of the sitting rooms on the ground floor. You could expect nothing better in the way of a hotel parlor, Leonidas reassured himself as the gloomy spaciousness together with its furnishings unaccustomedly got on his nerves. It's terrible to see the love of your life again in the public intimacy of this all-purpose lounge. Any bar would have been better, even a crowded coffeehouse with music. That Vera really and truly was the "love of his life" now gave Leonidas an unfounded feeling of security.

The room was filled with nothing but heavy pieces of furniture. They rose up into the unknown like the sullen fortresses of some lost garrison. They stood around like an auction deserted by the auctioneer, in which chance guests sauntering by ensconced themselves for a while or two: opulent sets of matching chairs and lounges, Japanese cabinets, light-bearing caryatids, an oriental fireplace, carved chests, end tables, and the like. Near the wall a grand piano stretched out chastely under a padded cover that draped it from top to bottom. Black, it resembled a bier for dead music. This pall was also weighted with all kinds of articles of bronze and marble arranged together as though for sale: a drunken statue of Silenius that balanced a calling card bowl, a supple dancer without a similar practical purpose, a splendid ink pot, large and serious enough to serve for the signing of a peace treaty, and so on, whose task it seemed was to prevent dead or seemingly dead music from escaping. Leonidas jumped on the suspicion that this piano was hollowed out, nothing more than a respectable fake since a

living instrument would have been used by the hotel man-
ager for the daily tea dance, which could be heard setting up
outside. The only living things in the room were a pair of
unfolded card tables with their bridge hands still spread
out. It made for a picture of comfortable distraction and
peace of mind that attracted Leonidas's envious glance
again and again. He was a master of this game of course . . .

He paced steadily back and forth, having to negotiate
himself around the sharp foothills of furniture and tables.
He still held the roses wrapped in tissue paper in his hand,
even though he felt the sensitive blooms were beginning to
wilt from his body heat. But he did not have the will to put
them aside. The weak fragrance traveled with him and made
him feel better. In his constant back and forth he could tell:
My heart pounds. I can't remember the last time my heart
beat so loud. This waiting really excites me. – He could also
tell: I've not a single thought in my head. This waiting fills
me completely. It's not clear yet how I'll begin. I don't even
know how I'm to address Vera. – And finally: She's making
me wait a long time. No minister has ever made me wait
this long. It's been twenty minutes at least that I've been
walking back and forth in this horrible lounge. I won't look
at the clock, not under any circumstances, so I won't know
how long I've been waiting. Naturally it's Vera's right to
make me wait as long as seems appropriate to her. Truly, a
small punishment. I can't even imagine how she waited in
Heidelberg, weeks, months, years . . . He didn't interrupt his
going in circles. In the ballroom the dance music throbbed.
Leonidas winced: *Oh not that!* It might be best if she did not
come at all. I'll wait here calmly for a full hour, even two,
and then go away without saying a word. I'll have done my
part and reproach myself no more. Hopefully she's not

coming. And it might be more than a little unpleasant for her to see me again. For me it feels like just before a serious examination, like surgery . . . So now a half hour has certainly gone by. I have to assume she left the hotel to avoid me. Well, I'll wait out my hour. This jazz racket is not so bad after all. It seems to make the time pass. And it's getting dark too . . .

The third number was underway outside when suddenly the small, delicate lady stood in the lounge.

"I had to make you wait," said Vera Wormser without justifying this sentence with any apology and extending her hand. Leonidas kissed the fragile hand in the black glove, smiling enthusiastically, mockingly, and beginning to rock on the balls of his feet:

"But please," he said with a nasally patronizing tone, "it doesn't matter at all . . . I've made a day of it . . ." And he cautiously added: "my dear lady."

With that he handed her the bouquet without taking off the paper. With a calm grasp she freed the tea roses. She did this attentively and allowed herself time. Then she looked around the grotesque room for a container. Immediately finding a vase and a pitcher of drinking water standing on one of the card tables, she filled the vase carefully and arranged the roses one after the other. The yellow flickered in the twilight. The woman said nothing. The little project seemed to occupy her completely. Her movements were composed from within, as so often is the case with the nearsighted. She carried the vase with the soft roses to the seats by the window, she placed them on the round table in the middle of them, and settled herself, with her back against the light, in a corner of the sofa. The room was changed.

84

Leonidas also sat down after he, with a meaningless, school-boy bow, had asked for permission. Unfortunately the white, fog-like cast of the late afternoon in the window made it impossible to see.

"My dear lady requested ..." he began in a voice that even disgusted him, "I received your letter only this morning and at once ... at once I ... Of course, I am totally at your disposal ..."

Only a little while passed before an answer came from the corner of the sofa. The voice was still bright, still child-like, and still seemed to have retained that dismissive air:

"You did not have to bother in person, Herr Section Chief," said Vera Wormser, "I hadn't expected it ... A telephone call would have been enough ..."

Leonidas made a motion with his hand, partly apologetic, partly frightened, like he wanted to say he was obligated to the dear lady under any circumstances to cover far greater distances than those from the Ministry of Culture and Education at Minorite Square to the Park Hotel in Hietzing. Here the not quite lively conversation broke off and Vera's face entered its first phase. Not only had the remembered image of his beloved been disturbed in Leonidas for years, his bad, astigmatic eyes, especially in gloomy rooms and impassioned moments, only revealed the blurred surface of what was seen at first. As yet Vera still had no face, only her delicate form in a gray traveling outfit from which a lilac silk blouse and a necklace of dark gold spherical pieces of amber vaguely stood out. So delicately girl-like was this shape, but only seeming to be "girl-like," belonging to a person of a tender, indefinite age whom Leonidas would not have recognized as his beloved from Heidelberg. Vera's face now began to penetrate the empty, bright surface, indeed as though from a far off distance. Someone seemed to be inexpertly screwing the thumbwheel of a telescope back and forth to get some distant object into sharper focus. It was something like this. First the hair appeared in the still blurry lens, that night-black hair, combed down to a gloss, and parted in the middle. (If one rested his eyes there, were those gray threads and strands running through it?) Then the eyes broke through, of this cornflower blue, shadowed, as before, by long lashes. Serious, inquisitive, and surprised they remained directed at Leonidas. The rather generous mouth held a severe expression, like one sees in women who have long practiced a profession and whose trained minds are seldom crisscrossed by trivial fantasies. What a contrast to the pouting fullness that Amelie's lips so often knew how to assume. Suddenly Leonidas realized that Vera had not made herself beautiful for him. She had not used the time that she made him wait to "fix" herself up. Her eyebrows were not plucked and penciled (Oh, Amelie), her lids not darkened with blue eye shadow, her cheeks not rouged. Perhaps her mouth had come in contact with a little lipstick. What had she been doing during the hour he waited? Probably staring out the window, he thought.

Vera's face was now finished, and Leonidas still did not recognize the forbidden image. This face resembled only an approximate reproduction, a translation of the lost countenance into the foreign language of another reality. Vera was calmly and persistently silent. But he, anything but calm, made an effort in continuing the "conversation" and finding what he called "the appropriate tone." He did not find it. What tone would have suited such an encounter? With horror he heard that nasal voice again imitating a vulgar aris-

tocrat who with impertinent certitude shows himself equal
to the most painful situation:

"Dear lady, you'll hopefully be staying with us longer
this time . . ."

After these words Vera regarded him in yet another shade
of wonder. She is surprised now at how she could ever be
taken in by so insipid a subject as me. Her presence has
always tested my weakness. His hands were cold with dis-
comfort. She answered:

"I am only here for two or three more days, until I have
everything settled . . ."

"Oh," he said with almost a note of fear, "and so, dear
lady, you're going back to Germany again?" He could not
conceal a bit of relief trailing off in the cadence of this question. Now he saw for the first time that the smooth, elfin-
boned forehead of the lady was completely furrowed with
straight lines.

"No! Entirely to the contrary, Herr Section Chief," she
retorted, "I am not going back to Germany . . ."

Something in him recognized her voice now, the pert,
implacable voice of the fifteen-year-old at her father's table.
He made a gesture of apology, as though to avoid some
unforgiveable slip of the tongue:

"Pardon me, dear lady, I understand. It has to be unpleasant now to live in Germany . . ."

"Why? For most Germans it is very pleasant," she noted
coolly, "just not for us . . ."

Leonidas took a patriotic approach:

"Dear lady, you should consider here, moving back to
your old homeland . . . We're starting to make things happen now . . ."

The lady seemed to be of another opinion. She declined:

"No, Herr Section Chief. I'm only here for a short time and can't presume to pass judgment. But we too would like to breathe the clean free air eventually . . ."

So there it was again, that old pride of these people, that infuriating presumption. Even then, when you had them locked in the cellar, they act as if they're looking down on us from the seventh floor. The only ones who are really their match are primitive barbarians who won't be discussing anything with them, but rather will club them down without further ado. I should call Spittelberger today and sacrifice this Abraham Bloch to him. *Clean free air.* She's virtually ungrateful to me. Leonidas felt the opprobrium and annoyance moving through his heart as anodyne. It relieved him a little. Meanwhile the face of the lady in the corner of the sofa reached a new phase, indeed, the final one. It was no longer a reproduction or rendering, but rather the original herself, albeit more intense, darker. And see, it still retained that harsh light of purity and strangeness that had once driven the poor tutor and later the young husband of another over the edge. Purity? No thought behind this white brow, you could tell, was not in accord with her entire being. She just showed herself to be stronger and more content than before. Strangeness? Who can express it? The strangeness had become stranger even if less sweet. The dance music blared up again. Leonidas had to raise his voice. An odd compulsion formed his words. They sounded dry and stilted, from one uncomfortable in his skin:

"And where, dear lady, do you intend to relocate?"

For her answer Vera seemed to draw a deep breath:

"I am in Paris the day after tomorrow and on Friday I board my ship in Le Havre . . ."

"So, dear lady, you are traveling to New York," said

Leonidas without a question mark and nodded approvingly, indeed, enthusiastically. She smiled weakly as though it amused her that even today she had come to disagree with everything, for thus far she had to preface nearly every one of her replies with a "no."

"Oh, no! New York? God forbid, that's not so simple. I don't have such high hopes. I'm going to Montevideo . . ."

"Montevideo," beamed Leonidas with an absurd tone, "that is terribly far."

"Far from where?" Vera asked calmly. She quoted that melancholy jest of exiles who lose their geographical point of reference.

"I'm a diehard Viennese," confessed Leonidas, "I mean, a diehard Hietzinger. It would take real resolve for me to move to another district. A life down there on the Equator? I'd be desperately unhappy despite all the hummingbirds and orchids . . ."

The woman's face in the twilight became a degree more serious.

"And I'm very lucky that someone offered me a teaching position in Montevideo. A large college there. Many envy me. We have to be very content when we find a place of refuge and even some work . . . But all this must be of no interest to you . . ."

"Of no interest," he interrupted her taken aback. "Nothing in the world interests me more . . ." And he closed softly: "I cannot tell you how much I admire you . . ."

This time it is no lie. *I really do admire her.* She has that incredible nerve and that damn independence of her race. What would become of me if I were at her side? Perhaps something would have really come of me. Something other than a section chief on the verge of retirement. But then we would not have gotten along for one single hour. His unease continued to grow. Suddenly something different, brighter pushed its way into the room, another room, where they stayed in Bingen, on the Rhine. – *Everything's in place, my faithful one, I see the old tile stove.* It was like the scales had fallen from the eyes of his memory.

"What's there to admire?" Vera said annoyed.

"I mean, you leaving everything behind here in the Old World where you were born, where you spent your whole life . . ."

"I am leaving nothing behind," she answered dryly. "I'm alone, I am not married fortunately . . ."

Was this a new burden for the scales? No. Leonidas sensed in this "I am not married" a final triumph that ran tingling through his veins. He leaned far back. To make further conversation was no longer necessary. The words faltered a little from his lips.

"I believe you have this young man to provide for . . . At least that is how I understood your letter . . ."

Vera Wormser suddenly brightened. Her attitude changed. She leaned forward. Her voice seemed flushed with excitement:

"If possible, would you help me in this matter, Herr Section Chief . . ."

Leonidas was silent a long while before it came from inside him warmly, deeply, without any self-consciousness:

"Why Vera, that's understood . . ."

"Nothing in the world is understood," she said and began taking off her gloves. It was like a small concession, like a gesture of good will, to go one step further and reveal a little more of herself. And now Leonidas saw the small, overly tender hands, each a trusting partner of that hand-in-hand once upon a time. The skin was a little yellowish and the veins stood out. On no finger a ring. The voice of the man quivered:

"It's obvious a hundred times self-evident, Vera, that I will fulfill your wish. I can place the young man in the best high school here, at the Scottish School, if that's all right with you. The semester has hardly begun, he can join the graduating class the day after tomorrow. I'll mind him, I'll take care of him, as best I can . . ."

Her face came still nearer. Her eyes lit up:

"You would really do that? . . . Ah, that makes it much easier for me to leave Europe . . ."

His otherwise perfectly composed face fell apart completely. He had the eyes of a begging dog:

"Why do you shame me this way, Vera! Don't you see what it looks like to me . . ."

He moved his hand close to hers resting on the table, but he dared not touch it:

"When will you send the boy to me? Tell me something about him. Tell me his first name . . ."

Vera gave him a wide look:

"His name is Emanuel," she said hesitantly.

"Emanuel? Emanuel? Wasn't your late father named Emanuel? It's a beautiful name, not overused. I'll expect to see Emanuel tomorrow at eleven-thirty, that is, at the Ministry. It will not come without being challenged. It will even be the most difficult challenge. But I am prepared to take it on, Vera. I'm prepared for the most drastic decisions . . ."

She seemed suddenly to become cool and to withdraw again:

"Yes, I know," she said, "someone has already told me about these obstacles that are placed in the way of people, even with the best connections now . . ."

He hadn't really listened. His fingers were knotted together:

"Don't think about these difficulties. You have no reason to believe my pledge, but I give you my word, this matter will be arranged . . ."

"You have the power, after all, Herr Section Chief . . ."

Leonidas lowered his voice as though he wished to convey a secret:

"Tell me, tell me about Emanuel, Vera. He has to be talented. He couldn't be otherwise. What is he good at?"

"In the natural sciences, I believe . . ."

"I would have thought that myself. Your father was a great scientist. And how is Emanuel, I mean, outwardly, what does he look like . . ."

"He doesn't look," answered Fraulein Wormser with a certain brusqueness, "as though he would make a scandal of your patronage if that's what you're afraid of, perhaps . . ."

Leonidas looked at her without understanding. He kept his fist pressed against his stomach, as though that would master his excitement:

"I hope," he gasped, "that he looks like you, Vera!"

Her look slowly filled with comprehending amusement. She prolonged the uncertainty:

"Why should Emanuel look like me?"

Leonidas was so moved that he whispered:

"I was convinced all along that he is your very image . . ."

After enjoying a long pause, Vera said at last:

"Emanuel is the son of my best friend . . ."

"The son of your best friend," stammered Leonidas before he grasped it. Outside the music started into a swinging rumba, too loud. A terrifying hardness spread across Vera's features:

"My friend," she said and one would have noticed that she forced herself to remain calm, "my best friend died a month ago. She had outlived her husband, one of the most important physicists, by only nine weeks. They tortured him to death. Emanuel is their only child. He was entrusted to me . . ."

"That's horrible, just horrible," Leonidas broke the brief silence. But he felt none of this horror in the least. Instead, an incredible astonishment filled him and gave way to realization, then this indescribable relief: I have no child with Vera. I have no seventeen-year-old son I must answer for to Amelie and to God. Thank heaven! Everything remains in the past. All my fear, all my suffering today were just bad dreams. I've run into a jilted lover after eighteen years. Nothing more. A difficult situation, half awkward, half tragic. But to speak of *inexpiable guilt*, that would be an exaggeration, your honor. I am no Don Juan among men. It was the only affair of its kind in an otherwise irreproachable life. Who'd throw the first stone at me? Vera herself doesn't give it a thought anymore, this modern, independent, radically progressive woman who's in the middle of a busy life. She's happy I didn't come back for her that time . . .

"Horrible, what's going on these days," he said again but it sounded almost like rejoicing. He jumped up, bowed over Vera's hand and pressed his burning lips to it in a long kiss. He was at once full of musical eloquence.

"I give you my sacred promise, Vera, that your poor

friend's son will be cherished as if he were your son, as if he were my son. Don't thank me. I have you to thank. You've made me a most merciful gift . . ."

Vera did not thank him. She said nothing. She stood there in an attitude of getting up, leaving, as if she wanted to prevent this conversation from trespassing a sacred boundary. It was already quite dark in that overstuffed lounge. Those monstrosities of furniture melted into formless masses. The false twilights of this rainy October day had been followed by the real twilight of evening. Only the tea roses still radiated a constant light. Leonidas felt the smart thing to do was make a getaway. Everything sayable was said. Any further step must lead to a moral cliff of loose stone. Vera's strange rigid bearing forbid alluding to anything sentimental. The simplest "tact" required the immediate parting ways and advised not doing so on a heavy note. Since this woman had crossed this episode out of her life, why should he even bring it up? On the contrary he should be pleased that the dreadful hour had passed so leniently and rapidly sought a worthy conclusion. Leonidas warned himself in vain. He was much too aroused. The luck of knowing this release from the ruin of his life flowed through him like recovery, like rejuvenation. He no longer saw the small delicate lady of his agonized conscience before him, that rediscovery of an old debt, but rather a Vera fully present whom he no longer feared. Since the need to change his life had receded, the consummate arrogance that he had lost this morning shot back into his nerves – and with it a short-winded, yet mad tenderness for this woman who had emerged like an apparition only to disappear eternally from his feelings of guilt, earnestly, nobly, and without making the least demands. He took her insubstantial hands and pressed them against his chest. Now was like picking up his adventure where he had so despicably left off eighteen years ago:

"Vera, dearest dearest Vera," he sighed, "I stand wretched before you. Words can't express it. Have you forgiven me? Could you forgive? Can you?"

Vera looked to the side, turning her head almost imperceptibly. How this infinitesimal deflection went on in his soul. Incomprehensibly, nothing was lost. Everything took place in a mysterious simultaneity. Her profile was for him a revelation. The daughter of Dr. Wormser, the girl of Heidelberg, was here in person, no longer obliterated from memory. And the gray strands, the resigned mouth, the lines in her forehead, they increased bittersweetly the fleeting ecstasy:

"Forgive," Vera took up his question, "that's a clichéd word. I don't like it. The things one has to regret, that you can only forgive yourself . . ."

"Yes, Vera, that is true a hundred times over. When I hear you speak this way, I realize what a singular creature you are. How right you were not to marry. Vera, truthfulness itself is too good for marriage. Every man would have to be a liar to you, not only me . . ."

Leonidas felt that lust of male irresistibility in himself. He would have had the courage now to seize Vera. But he chose to cry: "I've never forgiven myself and never will, not ever, never . . ."

But before he said anything he had already forgiven himself, for once and for all, and the guilt had been wiped from the chalkboard of his conscience. Therefore his statement sounded like joy. Fraulein Wormser pulled herself away from him with a slight movement of her hands. She picked up her purse and gloves from the table:

"I will have to go now," she said.

"Stay a few minutes, Vera," he whispered, "we'll never see each other again in this life. Give me something, anything to part on good terms, so I can look back like one fully pardoned . . ."

She still looked to the side, but she stopped buttoning her gloves. He sat down on the arm of a lounge chair so that he had to lift up his face to hers and came closer than he had thus far:

"You know, dearest dearest Vera that no day has gone by in the past eighteen years that I have not suffered silently like a dog because of you and me . . ."

This admission had nothing at all to do with truth and untruth. It was nothing but the lilting melodies of release and delicious nostalgia that filled him without getting in each other's way. Although her face was close, he didn't see how pale, how tired Vera suddenly looked. The gloves were buttoned. She held her purse under her arm already:

"Was it not better," she said, "to go separate ways?"

Leonidas, however, would not be interrupted:

"Did you know, my dearest, that I was thinking about you the entire day, hour after hour. You were my only thought since this morning. Did you know that I was totally convinced until a few minutes ago that Emanuel is your son and mine. And did you know, because of Emanuel, I was close, so close to going to a hotel, to asking my wife for a divorce, to leaving our charming home and starting a new, hard life when the door was about to close on this one? . . ."

In reply the woman echoed for the first time her old familiar disdain as though from some outer ring of profound weariness:

"How nice that you were only *close*, Herr Section Chief . . ."

Leonidas could not make himself stop. Eagerly it burst from him, his confession:

"For eighteen years, Vera, since that hour when I, for the last time, reached down to you from the window of my compartment, there was this persistent conviction in me that something happened, that we had a child together. There were times when this conviction was very strong, but it grew weaker over time until it was, every now and then, like a flame under the ashes. But it bound me inseparably, so far from you, as you might have suspected. My rotten cowardice connected me to you, even while it stopped me from looking for you, finding you. Surely you, Vera, haven't thought about me for years. But I have thought about you every day, even anxiously, with my conscience gnawing away. My unfaithfulness was the most enormous grief in my life. I've lived in a strange communion with you, I can finally admit it. Did you know that I had nearly torn up your letter this morning out of cowardice, just as I had torn up your letter unread that time in St. Gilgen . . ."

It was hardly out when Leonidas stiffened. Without intending it, he had exposed himself hip deep in the bottommost slime. A sudden feeling of shame, like a bristle brush, ran up back of his neck. Why had he not left in time? What devil had goaded him into this confession? His eyes were directed toward the window, beyond which the arc-lamps hissed upward. The mosquito dance of minute raindrops circled around the globes of light. Fraulein Vera Wormser stood motionless. It was entirely dark. Her face had taken on an even paler light. Leonidas felt the fading body, from which he looked away, as something priestess-like. The voice, however, cool and matter-of-fact, as it was in the beginning, seemed distant:

"That was very practical of you then," she said, "not to read my letter. I shouldn't have written it in the first place. But I was so alone and helpless during that time when the child died . . ."

Leonidas didn't turn his head. Suddenly his body was made of wood. The word "meningitis" grew up inside him. Yes, in that very year the epidemic had decimated so many children in the area around Salzburg. The event, for some unknown reason, had entrenched itself in his memory. Even though he was made of wood, his eyes began to tear. He felt no pain, only a kind of strange embarrassment and something more unexplainable that forced him to make a step toward the window. Thereupon the same clear voice grew more distant:

"He was a little boy," Vera said, "two and a half years old. He was named Joseph, after my father. It's unfortunate that I've spoken about him now. I had set out firmly resolved not to speak about him, not with you. For you have no right . . ."

The man of wood stared through the window. He thought he felt nothing but the hollow trickling away of the seconds. He saw deep into the earth of the village churchyard of St. Gilgen. A sad and lonely mountain autumn. There lay strewn apart in the moist black decay the little bones that came from him. Until Judgment Day. He wanted to say something. For example: "Vera, I have only loved you!" Or: "Would you try once more with me?" It was all ridiculous, stupid, and lying. He said nothing. His eyes burned. When he turned around, much later, Vera was already gone. Nothing remained of her in the dark room. Only the eighteen soft tea roses, which stood on the table, still retained what was left of their light. The fragrance, encouraged by the gloom, drifted up in mellow, faintly putrid waves, stronger than before. Leonidas was hurt that Vera had forgotten or rejected his roses. He picked the vase up from the table to bring them to the porter. At the door to the lounge, however, he reconsidered, and put the flowers of death back in the perfect darkness.

SEVENTH CHAPTER

Asleep

Leonidas stands behind Amelie in their loge at the opera. He bends over her hair, which thanks to her long ordeal under that nickel-plated helmet, surrounds her head like an immaterial cloud, a dark gold mist. Amelie's glorious back and her immaculate arms are bare. Only narrow shoulder straps hold up the velvety, sea-green velour of her gown, which she is wearing for the first time this evening. An expensive Parisian design. Amelie is in a festive mood as a result. In the glory of her self-assurance she expects Leon to be just as festive in light of her stunning appearance. She appraises him and sees an elegant man who wears a gray and crumpled face screwed on above the dazzling breast of his tuxedo. A fleeting shadow of dread falls over her. What has happened? Between lunch and the opera, has the eternally youthful dancer become a distinguished old man whose blinking eyes, whose sagging mouth barely suppress his boredom with life on this evening?

"Did you have a bad day, you poor man?" Amelie asks absentmindedly again. Leonidas works hard to force his dashing-mocking smile without bringing it to completion:

"Nothing worth talking about, my dear. Only one

meeting. Otherwise I spent the entire afternoon loafing around . . ."

She snuggles up to him with her marble-white back:

"Did my stupid speech upset you? Is it my fault? You are right, León. All this misery comes from hunger. But what can I do with thirty-nine coming on? I don't want to jiggle through life with a nice double chin, an upholstered chest, and two piano legs? You need to thank me, you beauty fanatic. Right now, don't tell anyone, I can barely wear a designer dress without making a few small alterations. I'm not lucky enough to be a skinny little stick puppet like your Anita Hoyos. You men are so unfair. If you would preoccupy yourself with me more, I wouldn't remain such uncontrollable trash, instead I'd be as tactful and sensitive and charmingly reserved as you . . ."

Leonidas makes a small dismissive gesture with his hand.

"Don't worry about it. A good confessor forgives his penitent children of their sins . . ."

"I don't think it's fair that you so quickly forgot that I was really hurt," she pouts, already turned around again, putting the opera glasses to her eyes.

"What a fine house this evening!"

It really is a fine house. Everyone with title and name gathered at the opera tonight. An important foreign dignitary is expected. A celebrated prima donna is making a public appearance before departing on her American tour. Untiringly Amelie tosses out her net of smiles, greeting everyone, and draws it in, dripping with the light of reciprocation. Like Helen from the walls of Troy she ticks off the assembled personalities, the order of snobbery in one excited report:

"The Chvietickys, orchestra pit box 3, the princess has

already smiled at us twice, why haven't you answered, Leon? Next to them the Bösenbauers, we have behaved terribly to them, we must invite them this month, a bridge party *en petit comité*, just the four of us, please be especially nice. Now the English envoy is looking over here too, Leon, you must acknowledge him. Sitting in the state loge is that impossible colossus, Spittelberger's wife, I think, she has a wool jumper on, what would you say if I dressed like her, you would not like that at all, so honor my hidden courage. The Torre-Fortezzas waved, how charming the young princess looks and she is a good three years older than me, I swear, Leon, you need to thank ..."

Leonidas turns grinning, making abbreviated bows in all directions. He greets everyone haphazardly, the way the blind do as someone whispers names in their ears of people they are meeting. Such are the Paradinis, it runs through his mind, but he forgets that he is no different than Amelie, pleasantly thrilled by the gush of illustrious names ... He reminds himself again and again to look happy because everything so unexpectedly, so splendidly resolved itself, because he can no longer be held to any serious admissions and decisions, in short, because his dark secret has disappeared off the face of the earth and he can be freer and easier than ever. Unfortunately he is unable to follow through with his invitation to this happy state. He even entertains the extravagant regret that Emanuel is not his son, a son he has lost. Oh, if only Emanuel were now a grown little Joseph Wormser who died of meningitis eighteen years ago in St. Gilgen. Leonidas can't help himself, a train is clattering in his head. And in this train Vera travels from a country where she cannot breathe to a country where she can. Who would ever think that in such countries, where these overbearing people can't breathe, highly skilled men like Emanuel's father are tormented to death for no reason? This is just another "atrocity" story. *I don't believe it.* Even if Vera's telling the truth, I don't want to believe it. But what is this? It seems as though I can't even breathe here. Why? Why can't I, someone with a blood right, breathe here? I thought I'd at least be allowed that. I better have my heart checked right away. Perhaps the day after tomorrow, in secret, so that Amelie doesn't find out. No, my dear colleague Skutecky, I will not make a pilgrimage to Herr Lichtl, to that triumphant mediocrity, but to Alexander (Abraham) Bloch instead without worrying about the bill. Beforehand, however, tomorrow morning, I should go see Vincent Spittelberger: Herr Minister, please accept my humble apologies for yesterday's difficulties. I've slept on those ideas of yours, Herr Minister, and you have rediscovered the egg of Columbus. I've brought along both the medal request for Professor Bloch and the appointment decree for Professor Lichtl. We must reflect on our national personality at last and assert it against international self-advertisement. Herr Minister, you are most expeditious and at today's cabinet meeting you can certainly get this paperwork signed by Herr Chancellor. – Thank you, Herr Section Chief, thank you! I never doubted for a minute that you're my one friend here. This is in confidence, if I move on to the chancellorship, I'm taking you with me as my Chief of Staff. Don't worry about yesterday. You were just a little under the weather. – Yes, of course, the weather. Stormy weather. Leonidas had the forecast in his ear. While getting dressed for the opera, he had switched the radio on: "Depression over Austria. Storms approaching." That's why he could not breathe. Leonidas is still nodding mechanically into the emptiness. He greets everyone well in advance to please Amelie.

Their guests, whom they had invited to the theater, had appeared. A tuxedo and a silvery black gown squeezed into an evening coat made out of some metal. The ladies embraced each other. Leonidas pressed a fat perfumed hand, speckled with brown liver spots, to his mouth. Where are you, fleshless hand, bittersweet hand with your fragile fingers without a ring?

"Dearest lady, you get younger every time . . ."

"If this goes any further, Herr Section Chief, you may introduce me as a baby next time. . ."

"What's new, dear friend? What's going on in high politics?"

"I have nothing to do with politics, thank God. I'm a humble educator."

"When you're being evasive, my dear Section Chief, then things must be going rather badly. I just hope that England and France will understand our situation. And America, before all America. In the end we are the last bulwark of culture in Central Europe . . ."

The words of his guests bothered Leonidas, he didn't even know why.

"Having culture," he said grimly, "expressed another way, is having gone to seed. All of us here have gone to seed, God knows. I don't count on the powerful, not on the big. The rich Americans happily come to Salzburg in the summer. But theatergoers are not allies. Everything depends on whether one is strong enough to change himself before the big change comes . . ."

And he sighed deeply because he didn't know if he were

strong enough and because that featureless sponge-face waxed before him full of hate.

Majestic applause. The foreign dignitary, surrounded by the natives, steps to the railing of the center box. The hall grows dark. The conductor, lit by the lone lamp on his lectern, suddenly tenses his profile and spreads the wings of an enormous vulture. Now the vulture flaps, making no headway, with regular beats above the unaccountably effusive orchestra. The opera begins. And I really enjoyed this once. A rather ample woman in the transvestite role jumps from the big four-poster bed of the ampler prima donna. Eighteenth century. The prima donna, an older lady, is sad. The male impersonator, her generous female form accentuated by her tomboyish prancing about, serves a cup of breakfast chocolate on a tray. Disgusting, Leonidas thinks.

On tiptoe he withdraws into the back of the private box. There he drops on the red velvet bench. He yawns deeply. It all came off smoothly. The problem with Vera is eliminated at last. An unbelievable creature, that woman. She didn't bring anything up. If the devil hadn't taken me for a ride again, had I not gone soft, I would have heard nothing, nothing, and we would have parted ways with dignity intact. Too bad. I was better off without the truth. No person can live two lives. At least I don't have the strength for the double life that Amelie thinks I'm capable of. She overestimated me from the very first day, my wonderful dear Amelie. Forget it, it's too late. I should never allow myself such tactless pronouncements again like those about the "big change." Change is for the birds. I'm not Heraclitus the Dark, not an intellectual Israelite, just a public servant with nothing to say from the mountaintop. Will I never learn to finally be a sheep like everyone else? One should always take heart in one's accomplishments. In this fine house the top one thousand have gathered. But I belong to the top hundred. I come from below. I'm one of life's losers. When my father died all too young, we, my mother and her five other children, had to live on a twelve-hundred gulden pension. When my mother died three years later, the pension was no longer there. I did not fail. How many are stuck at the level of being the Wormsers' tutor, never even realizing their bold dream to be schoolmaster of some provincial backwater, to sit in that little room pubs set aside for the village notables? And me? It's to my credit alone that I, with nothing but an inherited, ill-fitting tuxedo, was seen as a handsome young man, a famous waltzer, that Amelie Paradini insisted on marrying me, me of all things, that I'm not only section chief but a top man, and Spittelberger, Skutecky, and company know full well I don't need their business, I'm an exception to the rules, a nonchalant, and the Chvietickys, the Torre-Fortezzas, and the rest of that ancient feudal aristocracy smile across the way and say hello first – tomorrow at the office I will ring up Anita Hoyos and tell her I'm coming for tea. But first I'd like to know, did I really cry because of that little boy, or did I just imagine it afterwards . . .

Ever more heavily the music pulls itself over Leonidas. With long high notes the women's voices go at each other.

The monotony of excess. He falls asleep. But while he sleeps he dreams that he is asleep. He sleeps on the park bench. The October sun makes a weak appearance, sifting across the grass. Baby buggies are being pushed by in long columns. In these white carriages, which crunch across the gravel, sleep the consequences of causations and the causations of consequences with their bulging baby foreheads, protruding lips, balled-up fists, deeply preoccupied in their childhood sleep. Leonidas can feel his face feeling more and more like sand. I should have shaved a second time for the opera. A missed opportunity. His face is a vast arid plain. Slowly the paths, the cart trails, the approach roads to this lonely clearing grow together. If this is the sickness of death already, then isn't it nothing but the mysterious and logical correlation for the debt of life? While he sleeps under the oppressive dome of this continuously agitated music, Leonidas realizes with inexpressible clarity that today an offer was made to save him, dimly, with an undertone, indefinite like all offers of this kind. He knows he failed to take it. He knows that a new offer will not be made again.

SECOND CHAPTER
PAGE

11 *The Recurrence of the Same* – the title is taken from a major rubric in Nietzsche's metaphysics, which is, in part, satirized. The "eternal recurrence of the same" is that essential property that sets apart the Being of beings, those who embody the will to power, from all others.

12 *ad acta* – bureaucratic Latin meaning *filed, archived*.

17 *made them go away* – that is, flushed down the toilet. Readers of Werfel's day would understand the decorum of Leonidas having concealed himself in a bathroom.

18 *half-breeding* – from the German *Halbschlächtigkeit*, a term used by Kant (racial degeneration), Nietzsche (cultural degeneration), and Karl Kraus (the Viennese condition), and used figuratively to mean halfheartedness. Werfel intimates here that Leonidas's heart has "mixed" origins, hence his latent attraction to Vera.

THIRD CHAPTER

26 *Fairy Caprice* – a fairy godmother character who grants wishes to the capricious, such as the poor little girl in the nineteenth-century French morality play, *Blondine et la Fée Caprice*.

27 *a student of philosophy* – during the 1920s, the University of Heidelberg was the seat of the neo-Kantian school of philosophy.

29 *Rava Ruska* – in the context of Austria's national consciousness, a humiliating Austro-Hungarian defeat (September 3–11, 1914) at the hands of the Russian Army during the First World War.

29 *Traveler, if you go to Sparta* . . . – paraphrase of the famous epigram
by Simonides of Ceos on the lion monument at Thermopylæ:
Ὦ ξειν', ἀγγέλειν Λακεδαιμονίοις ὅτι τῇδε / κείμεθα, τοις κείνων
ῥήμασι πειθόμενοι (Go, stranger, and in Lacedæmon tell, / That
here, obeying her behests, we fell).

30 *lemur* – the rarely seen primate of Madagascar's forests that are
named for the evil spirit or animus of a dead ancestor that
haunted households in Roman mythology.

39 *Cavalier House* – Viennese slang for the Kaisersstöckl, a baroque
manse used as a lodge by the gentleman retainers of the Haps-
burg monarchy.

39 *Gloriette* – a colonnaded building and landmark on the grounds
of the Schönbrunn Park.

FOURTH CHAPTER

44 *end-in-itself* – a chief concept of Kantian morality vis-à-vis the
purpose of Humanity, corrupted here to mean that we never treat
bureaucracy (formerly "Humanity") as a means only but always
as an end in itself.

45 *Imperial Furniture Depot* – the Hofmobiliendepot on Andreas-
gasse is now the Vienna Museum of Furniture.

47 *Skutecky* – his Czech name and poor German casts him as an
inferior vis-à-vis real and prejudiced Viennese such as Leonidas.

49 *Spittelberger* – Werfel lampoons a stereotypical Austro-Fascist
politician of the 1930s, very likely Anton Rintelen, a Styrian jurist
and Christian Socialist politician who was twice minister of public instruction in the first Austrian republic. An ambitious man –
he was called "King Anton" by his admirers, including Alma
Mahler, who virtually pushed Manon Gropius at him. Rintelen
was the pretender to the federal chancellorship during the
abortive Nazi putsch of July 1934 that resulted in the assassina-
tion of Engelbert Dollfuss.

FIFTH CHAPTER

62 *burned hair and rubbing alcohol* – rubbing alcohol was once used
to clean curling irons.

64 *Pyramidon* – the trade name for aminopyrne, an analgesic invented in 1897 by Dr. Karl Spiro (a friend of Gustav Mahler and his wife) and manufactured by Bayer. By 1931 it was already banned in some countries for such toxic side effects as septic shock. The name Pyramidon is from the shape that caps on Egyptian obelisks, which, as an occult symbol, lent credence to the drug's infamous reputation. During World War II, high – and often fatal – doses of Pyramidon were administered at Dachau, whereas the German public was instructed to shun Pyramidon because it was invented by a Jew.

68 *seducer of servant girls on Sunday* – In Austria, as in other countries, servants traditionally have Sundays off for church, family, and their lovers. This insult is particularly stinging, for not only is caddishness implied, so is class, that Leonidas is socially no better than a servant's boyfriend.

70 *Jardin des Modes* – a French fashion magazine.

73 *Anita Hoyos* – a member of the Austrian nobility, the von Hoyos family.

SIXTH CHAPTER

77 *Volksgarten* – a public park in Vienna's first district.

79–80 *"If you could please . . . write down the name"* – honoring the subordinate's seemingly harmless request means more than it appears. The section chief's guarded reaction suggests that doing so can document an incriminating association with a Jewish woman.

80 *Herrengasse* – a street in Vienna's first district, where many of the former palaces of the Austro-Hungarian nobility had been transformed into government ministries.

85 *first phase* – Werfel, self-taught in Babylonian astrology, is alluding to the stations of the moon and by extension the myth of Endymion. Vera's association with moon is supported elsewhere in the text.

88 *primitive barbarians* – i.e., the Germans. Werfel satirizes how passive and civilized Austrian anti-Semites would welcome the Germans to solve the Jewish Question for them.

91 *Scottish School* – one of Vienna's elite schools.

SEVENTH CHAPTER

103 *egg of Columbus* – an expression based on the story of how Christopher Columbus made an egg stand on end to prove the earth was round. The story illustrates the notion that it takes genius to discover something new but that once it has been shown to others, then anyone can do it.

104 *bulwark of culture* – a conceit held by much of Austria's conservative, Catholic intelligentsia prior to the Anschluss.

105 *male impersonator* – i.e., Octavian in *Der Rosenkavalier* by Richard Strauss. This is the scene in Act 1 where Octavian serves "his" lover Marschallin in bed.

105 *Heraclitus the Dark* – Cicero's appellation for Heraclitus of Ephesus (fl. 6th century BCE), the pre-Socratic philosopher whose obscurity and complexity were designed to achieve multiple messages and thereby harmonize with the "signs of the World." Heraclitus's writings introduced the doctrine of Universal Flux (e.g., the paradigm of the river and its water) and the Unity of Opposites, which Werfel parodies in Leonidas's anxiety over changing his life and his attraction to his opposite, Vera – the Jewish Artemis of this novel. The temple of the Greek Artemis, the patroness of Ephesus, held Heraclitus's little book for much of antiquity.